Raise My
Ebenezer

RICHARD GERALD SHRUBB

RAISE MY EBENEZER

iUniverse books may be ordered through booksellers or by contacting:

*iUniverse
1663 Liberty Drive
Bloomington, IN 47403
www.iuniverse.com
844-349-9409*

*ISBN: 978-1-6632-2319-7 (sc)
ISBN: 978-1-6632-2321-0 (hc)
ISBN: 978-1-6632-2320-3 (e)*

Library of Congress Control Number: 2021913714

Print information available on the last page.

iUniverse rev. date: 07/08/2021

To the Ignatius J. Reilly in all writers. The less we recognize his presence, the more he has taken control of our minds. I hope he finished writing his book, found editors as qualified as mine, and finally published the thing, giving life to his characters and relief to his brain.

So the Philistines fought, and Israel was defeated, and they fled, every man to his home. And there was a very great slaughter, for thirty thousand soldiers of Israel fell …

When the Philistines heard that Israel had reassembled, the rulers of the Philistines came up to attack them. When the Israelites heard of it, they were afraid because of the Philistines. But that day the LORD thundered with loud thunder against the Philistines and threw them into such a panic that they were routed before the Israelites. Then Samuel took a stone and set it up between Mizpah and Shen. He named it Ebenezer, saying, "Thus far the LORD has helped us." So the Philistines were subdued and they stopped invading Israel's territory.

—1 Samuel, excerpted from chapters 4 and 7

Here I raise my Ebenezer;
Here by Thy great help I've come;
And I hope, by Thy good pleasure,
Safely to arrive at home.

—Robert Robinson, from "Come Thou Fount of Every Blessing," 1757

Contents

Prologue

I am through with my diary now. No one will read it, but I harbor a lingering stargaze that my writing may turn into something good—that someone will find my experience to be helpful. Even without renown, I take comfort knowing that God smiled upon Kevin Bruce and me as we wrote this diary. I gladly leave it at that. *Deus gignit artifex*; *Diaboli creat fama*.

It is Saturday night as I sit here in the screened porch on the back of my cabin, sipping rye whiskey with Phideaux. The women have left, and I am at my old writing desk, spotlighted in the darkness by my little green banker's lamp. Except for Phideaux, I am alone.

The hour is late, maybe even late enough on Saturday night that it is now early Sunday morning. If this is Sunday, then it is Easter Sunday. Judging by the feral quality of the women's singing while they walked out the door and up the path, they were happy. They were celebrating because I put my entire wealth into a donor-advised trust account supporting Sunday's church.

Sunday and the women were wonderful tonight. They were just what I needed, and I smile at the memory of them as I sit here reading my diary and petting Phideaux's ears. In addition to achieving my fact-finding goals about Ghibelline, the gathering was a delight.

I watch the pollen-clogged screens on my little porch breathe in and out as a million hungry insects push against them, trying to get through to eat me. I normally have more sense than to sit in bug-infested, witchy North Louisiana air so thick with pine pollen that it looks like a foggy mist, but I've probably not many nights remaining to live, so I choose to filibuster against life's mundane maladies and the commonsense behaviors designed to prevent them.

My duties are clear, for here I have taken my stand. Here, at this time and in this place, I raise my own Ebenezer. I embark tomorrow, Easter Sunday, beginning my quest to find and kill the creators and distributors of Ghibelline. *Vexilla Regis prodeunt inferni.*

CHAPTER 1

A Ronin in Limbo

Midway through this life of mine, I awoke to find myself in a
dark wood, where the right road was wholly lost and gone. How
I entered into it I cannot say, I was so full of sleep.
—Dante Alighieri, from *The Divine Comedy*, "Inferno," canto I

I intended to just go to the woman, retrieve her, and simply walk
her back into the restaurant to be with me, that's all, but it didn't
happen that way. The guy wouldn't let it happen that way. He
should have. It would have been in his best interest.

"What do you think you're doing?" he asked as I approached the
two of them in the parking lot. I didn't care about him, so I didn't
even bother to answer. I just stepped between them, put my arm
around the woman, and turned her away from him to begin walking
back to the restaurant with me. His anger heightened.

He grabbed my shirt. It was a rookie's mistake. We experienced
combatants know to either debilitate our opponents or keep our
hands to ourselves. While he was busy with my clothing, I bare-
knuckled him in the Adam's apple. At first he only bent from the
waist to gag a little, but soon he dropped to his knees, coughing,
and then he collapsed fully down onto his face in the parking lot,
convulsing. He wouldn't die, and I knew it, but still, he wasn't having
a very good day.

If I had quit at that moment, I could have just walked to my car
and driven away, as free as a bird. I know this to be a fact because

I have done it countless times before. Witnesses to violent events are so stupefied by what they have seen that they can't give useful information to the police, and that assumes that the police ever get called and people hang around long enough to talk to them once they arrive. Experienced killers like me are familiar with the phenomenon, and we use it to our advantage by barraging our opponents and then quietly slipping away into obscurity.

Oddly, I didn't do that; I stood over this guy, absentmindedly flatfooting him on the side of his face with the sole of my shoe. I remember making it a point to use my left foot and my right foot equally. Having ambidextrous skills is important for a martial artist, so I try to bear it in mind while I'm beating people. I do not allow a dominant-side skillset, because then the other side will grow increasingly weaker. In any situation, overinvolvement with one thing results in underinvolvement with other things. It goes that way every time.

When the police came and "apprehended" me, I told them I had kept my hands in my pockets the entire time I was foot-thumping the guy, but they failed to see that fact as an act of self-control. The other people in the restaurant had either left or developed a bad memory by then, so nobody stepped up to say, "He saved a woman." She was gone, too, by the way. I speculate that she and the guy may have had things to hide from the law, so while I'm sure she was grateful for what I did, she no doubt considered it in her best interest to not be there when the police arrived. I've learned enough about situations of abuse to know that sometimes victims stay silent because they're furtive, not because they're intimidated, which is probably why the guy didn't press charges.

There's a reason some sufferers stay under wraps, and I used it to my advantage quite a lot during my years as a hit man. The best time to attack people is while they're in a circumstance of compromised virtue. People who are wronged while they're at a whorehouse or a crack house tend not to report the incident to the police, and that tendency extends to buyers and sellers alike. It also applies to happenstance witnesses. The metaphor of whorehouses and crack houses extends into many, many things.

I was having lunch on the day of the incident in a town called Madisonville, Louisiana, which is a quaint little bedroom community on the other side of Lake Pontchartrain from New Orleans. It's only about an hour's drive from my condo in the city across the Causeway Bridge. I was in Madisonville because I was thinking about moving there. This all happened less than a year ago, in 2008. I am fifty years old.

The woman I rescued had been my server at the restaurant where I was having lunch, which is the sum total of how long I had known her. She was a delightful person—as adorable as she could be! She was an undergraduate student enrolled in the College of Education at Southeastern Louisiana University in Hammond. She wanted to be a kindergarten teacher.

The woman's cutest feature was her voice. It was babyish—exactly the kind I like. If ever there was a vocal doppelgänger for Butterfly McQueen saying, "I don't know nothin' 'bout birthin' babies, Miss Scarlett," then this woman would be it. I could have listened to her talk all day and liked it. I also enjoyed the way she smelled. It was a combination of pumpkin and vanilla, with maybe just a wisp of pine trees after rain on a cool day. I don't have any children, but if I did, I'd want this woman to be their kindergarten teacher.

She ended her shift while I was still eating, so we settled my bill and she topped off my cup of Community Coffee, and then she left for the day. I was quietly enjoying the coffee with a piece of buttermilk pie as she departed. Since I was on the patio, I could see her walking to her car. What she lacked in height she made up for by having many curves, and I was distracted by admiring them as she moved. Because of that, I didn't see the man at first. The coffee also had me a little distracted. It had chicory, and I was trying to decide how I felt about it as I ate my pie on the patio. In full disclosure, I should write that I was still pondering the taste of chicory as I thwacked the man's face with the sole of my shoe in the parking lot. I thought about telling that to the police but decided against it because it made me seem a little barmy. Back when I knew I was sane, I didn't worry about such things.

The guy who attacked the woman was apparently stalking her, and when she entered the parking lot, he confronted her. I was annoyed by the presumptive ease with which he did it. Such things have been bothering me lately—a lot more than they ever did in my youth.

I couldn't discern exactly what they were saying, but their voices were raised enough that I knew he was angry and she was alarmed. Before I could put down my coffee cup, he reached over and popped her on the side of her head. That was all I could take.

I eased quietly over the railing on the patio and went straight to the woman's aid. I didn't rush, but neither did I pause or linger. I intentionally used a smooth roll over the railing followed by a brisk pace. Having been six feet, two inches tall and athletic all my life, rolling over railings and walking briskly are fluidly easy for me. I did not yell or run at them. I walked calmly, for I did not want to add volatility to this situation by arriving demonstratively into it.

By the time I reached them, the guy had open-hand smacked my waitress a few more times, and all the patrons on the patio of the restaurant were watching the show. Glancing back over my shoulder at them, I saw nothing but bugged-out eyeballs and gaping mouths. I hate that look in people. It's a sign of weakness and stupidity.

Since I had no prior run-ins with the law, my sentence was probation and court-ordered therapy. As part of that therapy, I am going about the task of documenting my life's journey in this diary. My therapist tells me to call it a diary and not a journal, by the way. She says a journal is like a captain's log, meant to record factual data and measurable events during current activities to preserve details for future reference, but a diary is reflective and uses the past, present, and future as a through-line to establish thematic meaning. She says understanding the flow of my life over time will help with my anger-management difficulties. She has no clue. Good people usually don't.

My therapist's name is Dr. Patricia Virgil—Pat for short. Considering that I, too, have a PhD, we often speak to each other using our first names. I liked her from the start because she shares my clapback sense of ironic humor.

"Did anyone ever tell you that you look like Mariska Hargitay?" I asked her during one of our very first sessions.

"Yes, all the time, but it's ironic when you say it, since you look exactly like Peter Hermann."

"I hear that a lot," I said, "but why is it ironic?"

"Because they're married."

"Oh … I didn't know that."

"How could you not know? They're a famous Hollywood couple, and they're in the news all the time because of their charitable endeavors."

"Because I don't care about societal news. I never have. It's a flaw in my character." We paused in our conversation to laugh a little.

"Speaking of celebrities," Pat added with a thin segue, "I want you to think of one or two famous people who remind you of yourself, then explain why they make you feel that way."

"Do I have to pick the real people, or can I pick their characters?"

"Whichever you prefer."

I sat quietly for a few moments of reflective pause and then said, "Peter Hermann, because I look like him, and Jason Bourne, because I act like him."

"Why do you feel you behave like Jason Bourne?"

"Because he's dangerous, but in a hidden kind of way; and because he claims he wants out of his life of violence, but he has too many unanswered questions to just walk away." I looked at Pat as I finished describing my Jason Bourne reasoning, and I noticed she had a thoughtful look on her face.

"What's on your mind, Doc?"

"I get the reference to you being dangerous, but I think Jason Bourne is too controlled to parallel you." She paused and then asked me a question. "How would you feel if I said you're more like Martin Riggs from *Lethal Weapon*?"

"I'd want to know what makes you think that."

"Because he's a dangerous man in search of justice, but he's also more than a little self-destructive."

Unfortunately, I saw her reasoning. "Make me normal," I blurted without hesitation.

"We may have to settle for keeping you safe," she said in response.

I didn't know Pat before the judge "introduced" us. I guess she's about my age, but I could be mistaken. I'm a terrible judge of such things. Her look is plenitudinous but not overly feminine, which is my favorite aura in women; and she has dark hair, which is also my preference. Occasionally she wears glasses during our sessions. It is that triad which I find most attractive: sonsy, dark, and intelligent. She's also a zelig. It's a wonder I don't ask her to marry me.

I'm still young enough to have an active sex life, but I'm going through some sort of dry spell where women are concerned. Women to me now are good company, but I don't have any desire for them beyond mere companionship. That's probably why Pat can be everything I like in a woman and yet I don't act on that attraction. She is my therapist—nothing more.

Pat began our sessions by telling me that burnout is a situation of decayed attitude, and it causes people to do negative things that are outside the range of our normally positive behaviors. She also said burnout doesn't start with the day we first feel fatigued; it begins way before that, during a period of heightened celebration that makes us believe our future will be brighter than what we should reasonably expect to sustain. When things don't quite work out the way we had hoped, something within us turns sour. "The longer it takes to grow that expectation," Pat said, "the deeper the severity of burnout we experience."

It took me decades to nourish and grow my unrealistic expectations, so my emotional enervation and mental chagrin are running quite deep. I was a child of imaginary rainbows with an ardor of respect for all humanity. Pat tells me that this made for a bad start. She's right; thus my court-ordered therapy and the writing of this diary.

"Writing makes us stop and think," she said, "and it is that act of thinking which may help you see yourself from a different perspective. It's often helpful to pretend you're actually writing to someone conversationally, so consider using that style."

Pat also tells me that abnormally happy children are often hiding things which can come out during therapy. She cautions me to be prepared for these types of memories to surface. "It's a phenomenon called 'late processing'," she told me. "Dots begin to connect in your head to form a memory. Be aware that these memories can create feelings you've not had before, so be careful that you process those feelings without acting on them inappropriately. Write them in your diary, and we'll talk about them during our weekly sessions."

By the way, it's ironic that my arrest and court-ordered therapy are from the pounding I gave the guy in the parking lot, because that incident is among my most miniscule transgressions. It's is kind of like the way Al Capone went to prison for tax evasion but not for mass murder or international theft.

"Mark," Pat said to me during our first meeting, "as a woman, I appreciate what you did, but let's talk about ways you might have accomplished your goals differently." I snicker still at the memory of her saying that. Sometimes I laugh outright. "Let's talk about motivation," she added.

"Okay."

"What motivated you to do something so big for a total stranger?"

I paused before giving her a reply. "You're projecting," I said.

"How?" she asked. She seemed honestly baffled. I think she was a little surprised that I knew about the concept of psychological projection.

"Because since it would be difficult for you to intervene in that way, you're assuming it was a big deal for me. It wasn't. Considering my profession, putting a stop to that guy was the equivalent of asking a gourmet chef to make a peanut butter sandwich, except it didn't take me nearly as long or make as much mess."

I like watching Pat when I tell her things like this. She would be a horrible poker player, because her reactions are written all over her face. When she has a thought, her eyes get big, and when she has a feeling, she squints. As I gave her the gourmet-chef analogy, her eyebrows looked like they were doing push-ups.

"I just went over there to bring the woman back to safety," I continued. "It wasn't any more complicated or difficult for me than that simple intention." I could see Pat's mind was reeling. "Before I tell you more, let me clarify something. Are the things I say to you confidential?"

"Yes, totally, unless I learn that you're intending to harm someone. In that case, I'm required by law to inform the authorities. It's called the Tarasoff rule. As long as you talk about things from the past, I'm obligated to keep that information confidential, but equally, if you talk about harming someone in the future, I'm obligated to disclose that information. Legally, it's known as duty to warn."

"Does that include what I write in the diary?"

"Yes. The same standard applies. You don't even have to show me your diary unless you want me to read something specific. The benefit of that diary comes from the process of you writing it, not from the document itself. I only need to know of the thoughts and feelings it inspires, not the actual content."

After my descent into the deepest levels of corruption and darkness, I find it odd that I so willingly follow Pat's behest to talk and write. Considering all the hell and havoc I am now so capable of bringing upon other people, and all the piles of nebulous wealth I have accumulated through my evil deeds, for me to do this so compliantly is an interesting thing.

I'm taking my therapy seriously, and I need to commemorate that dedication here in these words. I have abnegated my lodestar, and I want it back! I worked my way into a life of decay one step down at a time, and now I'm trying to work my way up and out of it again the same way—spiritually and otherwise. One may not merely French exit a lifetime of bad habits and expect to get rid of them; we must kick the shit out of them before our departure. A clean break from diablerie requires sustainable intentionality. There's a difference between quitting something and simply not doing it anymore, and I'm on a determined path to actively repent and redeem my degenerate life. "Extirpate" would not be too strong a word.

During that first session, Pat kept dwelling on the woman at the restaurant. I expected her to get stuck on the man, but she hardly mentioned him. It was masterful.

"I'm not a combatant myself," she said, "but one thing I do know about warriors is that your greatest weapon is an element of surprise. With that in mind, even though it was not difficult for you to assist that woman, you still did it at risk to yourself. Your superiority notwithstanding, the guy could have pulled out a gun and shot you, and you at least made yourself vulnerable by exposing your talents. You're experienced enough to know these things, yet you helped her without hesitation, and even more interesting to me, you remained on the scene until the police arrived." Pat paused to think at that point, and then continued. "Did you know her before you met her as your waitress at the restaurant?"

"No," I said. As terse as that reply appears in writing, I feel a need to point out that I spoke the word calmly and somewhat softly at the time. I was in a relaxed and thoughtful mood.

"Does she remind you of a woman you love?"

"No," I replied, still with the same slow, placid tone of voice.

"Did you see her again?"

"No."

"Do you want to?"

"No."

Pat paused and looked at me hard. "I'm going to ask you again, but this time please linger to think before you reply. And by the way, please don't view our conversations as a contest to outwit me. I'm here to help by directing your thinking in new ways. Okay?"

"Okay."

"Please tell me, thoughtfully—why did you assist that woman?"

I considered my answer. "I didn't really think about it at the time. I just did it." I spoke the words in an almost dreamlike state.

"That seems unlikely for someone of your background and caliber," Pat said. "It just doesn't add up. You did a high-profile thing for no good reason, and then you lingered over this guy, cat-and-mouse style, pawing at his face with the bottom of your shoe until the police came." She paused. "Why were you in Madisonville in the first place, and what was your frame of mind?" Seeing these words on the page, I realize this makes her sound more formal and officious than what actually occurred, for her tone was slow and relaxed, like mine.

"I want to go into a kind of retirement," I said unguardedly. "Madisonville is a nice, quiet place to live." That seemed to really mean something to Pat. She looked at me straight on and hard before she spoke.

"Is there someone there you want to live near?"

"No. I just like the place, and I feel good when I'm there."

"Is anyone going to move there with you?"

"No. I want to continue to live alone."

"Do you have any family nearby?"

"No. My family is in Ohio—what's left of my family, anyway." As I said the word "family," I scrunched my face and made air quotes with my fingers for emphasis.

Pat seemed to break her concentration a little when I said these things. She glanced at the timer on her desk, but I had the vague suspicion she did so to cover for her dropped poker face.

"Before our session next week," she added quickly, "I want you to consider that people in a phase of limbo will sometimes do things to shake up their lives. Entering retirement is an emotional time for people, especially for someone as young as you are, so I want you to think about why you want to slow down. And why in Madisonville. And did the woman you assisted do more to inspirit you than you're realizing? Was it just the woman you were defending, or did that situation represent something more? For instance, were you trying to establish a reputation for your new existence there?"

"Okay" is all I said. I was gaining trust and respect for her.

"And Dr. Anthony," she added in parting, calling me by my title and last name for emphasis, "men who see themselves as a paragon for all good things will sometimes unknowingly base their ideology on women—specifically female body parts that fit into Victoria's Secret products. Women and sexual mores are important, but they're not pathways to anything: not to God, not to greatness, and certainly not to a precept for living. Please reflect on this before our next session."

Turns out I was the one who had no clue. I underestimated her. Apparently I, the king of gaslighting, had met my compeer.

"That's quite a lot to hit me with while I'm walking out the door and my guard is down," I said. "Are you sure you don't have a warrior's instincts for surprise?"

She smiled. "I've read your files, and I know your religious background, and I also know the geographic region and socioeconomic status within which you were raised. In concert with each other, those things can create powerful folkways. Little factory towns in the hills can be austere places, even when the landscape is as beautiful as Ohio. I have expertise in this subject, Mark, and I recommend that you take my counsel seriously."

"I do," I said. Of all the words in all the world, I'm not sure why I picked those two particular words, but they certainly came out.

As unexpected as her parting comments were, they nailed me. Pat wasn't talking about my literal sexual activity or the unvarnished physicality of women; she was talking about the conceptual influence these things had upon me. She knew how I leaned upon them as a crutch to shape my guiding values. Now that I was in a phase of midlife change, I was unmasking those values once again, detox style. I had a lot to ruminate on.

But I don't want to get ahead of myself; the beginning is always the best place to begin, starting with the premise that if we want a little more help from God, then we should start doing things that God cares about for a change. Les grandes pensees viennent du coeur. This is not as easy as it sounds, for our semiconscious states have a gravitational pull that must not be underestimated. I want my theology and my praxis to align, but it's going to take some work.

Why did that man and woman in the parking lot trigger me? Could I really be capable of temporary insanity after all? Me, of all people? I do indeed feel myself slipping occasionally, and it's also true that I have lost faith in humanity, which is odd considering I started my career as a public schoolteacher—high school English, to be exact.

Taking into account the overarching degree of my life's change, nothing is unthinkable. My murderous abilities could very well overpower the few molecules of decency I have remaining and take total control of my behavior. I've certainly done god-awful things to a lot of people; that's true. But so far, except for the baby, I've done those things only to people who deserved to have such things done unto them.

I feel I have three options, and two of them are dire: heal myself, kill myself, or become the very monster I have spent my life and career eradicating. These three outcomes are very real. My therapy must be successful!

CHAPTER 2

Martha in the Kitchen

As one by main force aroused, I awoke out of the slumber that
had bound me, and I moved my eye about, gazing intent to satisfy
my wonder concerning the place wherein I found myself.
—Dante Alighieri, from *The Divine Comedy*, "Inferno," canto III

Pat was right about late processing and the memories that would resurface. She did not, however, prepare me for the impact with which they would hit me.

Not long after my therapy sessions began, I took my diary to a local library to write. I've decided to draft it longhand, by the way, so I bought an actual leather-bound diary. The thing is massive. It looks like one of those old-world Lutheran Bibles carried across the Atlantic Ocean by immigrants on a ship in the 1800s. I picked this diary intentionally because its ceremonial air inspires me to take my writing seriously, and I like to write in it in a library because libraries stimulate thinking.

That day in the library, I wanted to let my middle-aged mind drift back to my early days of innocence—to contemplate with intention the beginning of my life. I was intending to reminisce about a specific field trip with my classmates to an art museum because the event was significant, but while I was in the library thinking, a second flood of memories hit me unawares. This flood was equally significant—maybe even more so.

Regarding the field trip I intended to write about, I was eleven years old at the time, but I looked seventeen. I was a big kid for a seventh grader, tall and lanky, with a head of dark, greasy hair. My face was a mask of pimples under a pair of eyeglasses. I stood head-and-shoulders taller than my classmates, which is ironic because I was also nearly a year younger than most of them. I'm a December baby, a Sagittarian, so I was eligible to start school with all the other children who were born in my calendar year, even if they were born in January of that year. I was four years old when I started kindergarten. Most of my other classmates began at five, and that's not even counting the ones who started a year late or flunked a grade or two after that.

I'm dwelling upon this in such detail now because I received the treatment and expectations of someone who was older than my classmates even though I was, in fact, a year less developed cognitively. I see now that the disjuncture damaged me, particularly when my classmates' parents saw me as a thing of danger to their children. I was a sweet-natured soul in a big, ugly body. That's an unfortunate combination always, but even more when it happens to an impressionable young person. All in all, I think that period of childhood hardship helped me when I became an adult, because I had already developed a depth of character, but I had some tough going for a decade or so during my formative years. That kind of thing can be hard for a person to scrape off, and we tend to carry it around as part of our home bases of identity. I did.

Because I was so tall, I had a good view of the paintings in that museum while we ambled in a tight pack somewhat resembling a line—heavily supervised, of course. I was excited about the trip to the art museum. I'd never been to one before. I'd heard a lot about art, and I was eager to see some. My expectations were artificially high, and as my therapist has pointed out, I need to be careful of such emotions. I know that now, but I did not know that when I was eleven.

Inside of the museum, I studied the paintings. I knew they were certainly better than what I could do, but I was disappointed because I wasn't experiencing any magical moments.

We had been given a series of cautionary reprimands from our teachers, telling us that visiting a museum was a great honor and we needed to be on our very best behavior. I thought something that cost millions of dollars and was surrounded by that much preventive security should inspire an enchanted reaction, but I wasn't getting any. So far, I was just a tall, sweaty kid who was stuck in line among short, sweaty kids. A couple of years earlier, two of my cousins and I had stumbled upon a stack of girlie magazines, and we were still trying to recuperate. Now *that* was a magical moment! And those magazines were free and unguarded. Based on parallel reasoning, I thought that if pictures that were open and accessible gave me a mind-altering experience, then surely pictures that were expensive and enshrined would be miraculous.

Being inherently quick to blame myself, I thought that if I only worked harder at understanding the art in the museum, then my spellbinding, otherworldly experience was sure to come. Peter Pan said that if we believed hard enough, we could fly, and since Santa said the same thing about getting presents, I willed belief into my eyes and looked harder at the paintings. Surely the problem lay within me—or so my parents and Sunday school teachers had said.

In one particular painting, I saw a lot of small blocks on a large piece of cloth. The blocks weren't square and equal like those on a checkerboard; they were odd-shaped and of various sizes, yet still somehow equiangular. I thought maybe that was a clue to understanding the painting—all that precision and intention. I looked at their details. I guess I was about ten feet away from the painting when I first saw it.

Each of the small blocks seemed well done and very precise within itself. I thought that if I stepped closer, then I could make sense of the painting. I turned sideways from my line of classmates to face the painting, and I took a small, cautious step in its direction, from ten feet away to nine feet away, then another small step to eight, and then another to seven. Nothing mystical happened. I was careful to keep my hands in my pockets so nobody could accuse me of trying to grope the artwork. My group pushed me glacially to the side a little bit every time I took a step toward the painting. I inched to it again—six feet and counting down. Still nothing. Five feet now, and nothing. Slowly and carefully, I removed my hands from my pockets and moved them up my body to put them on my glasses. I kept my bony elbows tight to my ribs so I wouldn't alarm anyone as I tried adjusting my retroscopic tilt—no information. Pantoscopic tilt—even less.

I nudged up to the three-inch-thick red velvet rope between me and the painting. It was a line of morality I dare not cross. I put my hands back in my pockets.

My classmates were starting to complain. My teachers noticed the disruption, but it was not enough to single me out for an individual scolding. As they admonished the group to keep moving and not touch anything, I leaned over the velvet rope.

Like a kid at Christmas yearning to sustain my belief in North Pole magic, I struggled to perceive the thaumaturgy I hoped was in that painting. I hungered for a glimpse of the Big Deal, whatever it was, and I concentrated with all my might. My classmates nudged harder, bumping me and jeopardizing my balance. My teacher now rebuked me specifically. Mr. Minos was his name. He wanted the flow undisturbed. I remained steadfast on my tiptoes, my face thrust toward the painting, leaning over the rope farther and determined to keep my hands in my pockets in spite of my inclination to spread them for equilibrium. I was on a mission but was receiving nothing from the painting in return—no reciprocity at all.

I was already on thin ice with these people, so I didn't exactly start this day in a strong bargaining position. With my being freakishly bigger than my classmates, as I have already described, discipline and accountability seemed to land on me quite a lot. But the day in the museum was worse because I had recently given a book report that hadn't gone over well. I had done a good job during my speech, but the book itself was forbidden. All my classmates gave speeches from the required reading list, but I had a new topic.

We had a neighbor next door to my house who was an elderly German immigrant, and she told me a story once about being beaten in school for not reading *Mein Kampf*. Her story resonated so deeply with me that I decided to tell my classmates about her and give a report about that book. As I did not know that we were discouraged from reading *Mein Kampf*, my report didn't go well. Like her, I had deviated from normalcy. I kept hearing people on television tell youngsters like me that if we could only be brave and take chances, then we would be rewarded with success, but based on my empirical experience and real-life observations, I was beginning to believe those people were full of shit.

Still smarting from the failure of my recent book report, I pulled out of my stupor, leaned back onto my heels, turned to face in the same direction as my classmates, and moved languidly along with the same halting flow as everyone else. Order was restored.

During that entire half-minute event in the art museum, the only interesting thing that happened was my behavior, for it wasn't like me to demonstrate willpower. I usually stayed in line and did what was expected of me—by my teachers and classmates alike. Even velvet ropes controlled me with ease.

We continued toe to heel as an oscillating group, touring the museum. I appreciated the art, but I no longer had expectations of transcendence. I remained mindful of the people around me and only lackadaisically looked at the paintings. Children from affluent neighborhoods might be able to concentrate fully on their lessons and opportunities in school, but children from backgrounds like mine pay most of our attention to other people. True, it's an act of survival, but it's also an act of laziness. Nothing in the world is easier than neglecting our work to watch other people. I would like to believe that I kept this insight in mind during those years when I was a teacher, but the truth is I think I just got my reports and lesson plans turned in on time.

From my vantage point of being taller than the other kids in the museum, I could see artwork from wherever I was in the room. I could see paintings we were approaching as well as paintings we were departing. That's when it happened. From across the museum and out of the corner of my eye, I saw the painting I had been studying.

This time, having a visual gap and a clear mind not thinking about it at all, the painting was bewitching! I saw it! *Really* saw it! Once I started to see it, I couldn't stop seeing it. My mind had learned a new skill. For the next period of spellbinding moments, there was nobody in that museum but me. It was wonderful.

The painting made perfect sense, and all its parts came together. It was a picture of a single person, and on the person's face were two people, one male and one female. The person's forehead was made up of a lot of symbols and acrostic words and other people. I moved my focal point from one part of the painting to another, and each time I did, I saw a different image in my peripheral vision. Sometimes the image of the person took up the whole painting, but other times the person was small compared to all the other elements. Once, the background was even made up of what looked like us kids, right then and there in the museum, furniture and artwork and everything, but that would have been impossible. Right?

My brain locked onto the painting, and I wondered about the artist. Whoever it was, that person hadn't created this painting alone. Something had helped—something electrifying and inspiring. Nobody paints that much detail on a mere whim, so whatever that inspiration was, it must have been relentless and lasting. I yearned for a calling like that.

That experience is one of the worst things that could have happened to me, for I had accomplished a rapture, and I've spent too many years of my life trying to recapture that epiphany. Ever since then, I've designated at least a part of my brain at all times to a search for greater meaning, as if I were above my own reality, preferring divination over actual living.

I can't blame all my weirdness on that painting alone. I think I've always been a little berserk. Not batshit crazy, but just a little irregular. I prefer to think of myself as unparalleled and oblique, but lately I catch myself arguing with the television and losing to the commercials.

The trip to the museum was the memory I went to the library to intentionally explore and document in my diary. The other memory

I mentioned, the one that hit me by surprise, happened because I saw an interaction between a man and a woman in the library, and it made me recall something from my youth. That recollection started a chain reaction of other memories—important memories.

To an untrained eye, what the man and woman did in the library was nondescript. In fact, it was their intentional uneventfulness that attracted my attention. It was a little too uneventful, and in the spirit of it-takes-one-to-know-one, I noticed.

I was leaning back in my chair in a corner of the lobby and staring vacuously in the general direction of the checkout desk as I reflected on the painting in the museum from decades earlier. A woman in the library was lingering there by the checkout desk, but in a library, it's common for mothers to lingeringly wait for their children, so I didn't notice her much until the man entered the scenario. He at first simply walked past her, but then he came back. They looked at each other, and then he said something, she nodded, and he turned away and left. The entire exchange lasted about four seconds, literally, but I could tell by their body language that there was a lot of corroboration in that brief interaction; and since any depth of communication requires a lot of talking, I induced that they must have confabulated ahead of time. There's nothing wrong with any of this except that these two people clearly wanted minimal interaction in public, which is a red flag of conspiracy. About a minute later, the woman left too.

At first I chuckled to myself and dismissed the incident from my mind. After all, who was I to judge them? My superiority was that of mastery, not morality. I was better at dead-drop transactions than these two amateurs, but I was not a better person.

Across the lobby from where I was sitting, and behind a half-glass wall, there was what appeared to be a class of schoolchildren having a reading lesson during a field trip. I pleasantly watched them. Having come to the library to reflect upon my own childhood field trip, I was in a state of mind to recognize the group's purpose. My thoughts about the man and woman with their brief communication merged with the teacher reading to the children. That's when the late processing wrecking ball hit me. My father had done that exact thing with my eighth-grade teacher!

My eighth-grade teacher's name was Miss Helen. I think it was her first name, but she was so young and sweet that she let us call her Miss Helen. Some of my classmates called her Cleopatra, but I was too much in love with her to call her that. She had a boyfriend named Tristan. Lord, how I hated that man for being her romantic liaison! Little did I know that by this yardstick, I should have hated my father even more. At least Tristan was aboveboard.

My father took me to school one day, which is a thing I was too young to notice as being out of rhythm with his normal absentee-parenting behaviors. I was just pleased to be getting a little positive time with the guy, so it didn't occur to me to wonder why he suddenly cared about how I got to school. Decades later, I learned through my work as killer that a break in normalcy like that one is our greatest clue that something noteworthy is happening.

My dad insisted on walking me all the way to the classroom, which was bad enough; but then, after he left, he came back to the door, which mortified me. Only kids who were in trouble had parents standing in the doorway of our classroom, so by that reasoning, I believed I was in terrible trouble because my dad stood there twice.

When I got home, I tearfully told my mom. All hell broke loose, confirming to my clueless mind that I was indeed in trouble. I was too young and simpleminded to know that commotion like that doesn't happen because a kid tells one teary-eyed story—it happens because a wife's suspicions get spontaneously verified by an unsolicited scoop.

Fear makes us remember things, so my father's return to the door that day to say something to Miss Helen stuck with me. It was exactly like that of the man and woman in the library, right down to their overintentional air of casual ease. My father looked at Miss Helen, he said something, she nodded, and he turned away and left. Looking back through the lens of my experienced-adulterer understanding, I recognize that they were quickly verifying previously communicated details.

It was because of that one small exchange between the man and woman in the library that I remembered many things about my eighth-grade year. Miss Helen left midway through that year, and I was heartbroken. My friends punched me for her departure and told me it was my fault, and the school principal admonished me not to talk about it. I thought she was telling me not to talk about getting punched, so I didn't. I also remembered the way my father would drive down an out-of-the-way street in our town for no apparent reason, but I later learned that was where Miss Helen lived. I was walking on that street with my classmates one day when we saw her on her porch talking to Tristan.

"Well, if it isn't little Mr. Anthony," she said to me. I was stargazed that she knew who I was.

"Hi, Miss Helen. I didn't think you'd remember me."

"Oh, I remember you. I remember your father too."

"You know my dad?"

"Yes, and I know your mother too. Tell them I said hello."

"Okay," I said, genuinely perplexed. Tristan looked at Miss Helen, and they exchanged smirking glances between each other. I was already feeling vulnerable with my heightened emotions, so I noticed even these small details. Tristan shook his head, looked away, and busied his hands.

Later that day, I obediently told my mother Miss Helen said hello.

"When did you see her?!" my mother barked in interrobang surprise, spinning to straight-on face me as she spouted the words.

"I saw her at her house today."

"Why did you go to her house?!"

"I didn't. I was just walking by with my friends, and we saw her on her porch."

"You stay away from there and stop talking about her! Don't even think about her!" Exchanges like this made me grow increasingly silent with my parents. They confused me. If talking made them mad enough to bark at me, then clearly I shouldn't talk. I withdrew.

"Okay" is all I said to my mom, relieved that her aggression was only verbal.

I'm guessing Miss Helen told Tristan she had been falsely accused, but piecing together all the memories I have of my father's peculiar behavior and his knowledge of where she lived, that would make her a liar. I remember also her halo-and-horns treatment of me in her classroom. Influenced primarily by feelings of guilt, as I tend to be, I thought her fluctuating behavior was either because of things I was doing wrong or because of things I was not doing right enough. I now speculate that she was kind to me when she was happy with my dad and she was harsh with me when she was angry with him. That's a tough process for a kid with a crush to endure from the apple of his eye. She even hugged me once and told me I was her favorite, quickly admonishing me to keep quiet about it. Miss Helen must have been very pleased with my father that day.

I would write more about the significance of what all this did to me, but I honestly don't have the words. I'm pretty sure my mother would have killed Miss Helen if she had known about her peak-and-valley treatment of me in the classroom. Either that or she would have told me to sit down for a nice sandwich and forget about it all. It could have gone either way.

"Do you ever feel misogynistic?" Pat asked me when I told her the story about my mom, my dad, and my eighth-grade teacher.

"A little bit sometimes, but it's unsustainable." Pat laughed when I said that. "I do, however, enjoy a full-blown belly laugh at the notion that this is a man's world," I added. "*That*, my female friend, is the best-played poker hand of all time." Pat smiled with her eyes when I added these last words, but she did not laugh outright this time. "Keep writing in your diary" is all she said in reply.

By the way, I have something else I should be sure to mention: through this diary-writing effort, I've made a new friend. He's imaginary, but I still like him. His name is Kevin Bruce. If it is true that my world is a theater and all the men and women in it are merely players, then Kevin Bruce is my stage director. He's my muse. I'm not sure who painted the cubist picture I saw in the museum as a kid, but I'll bet the artist had a pestering muse like Kevin Bruce.

Quite a lot of my therapeutic mending process involves catechizing my own stereotypical thinking, and Kevin Bruce's very identity helps inspire this examination. For starters, I have been led to believe that all muses are the same: ballerina-like in appearance. They are thin, graceful creatures every one, eternally young, and moving with footsteps that can be described only as quick and light. And muses are female, dwelling ethereally above ponds of clear, clean water in sub-rosa sylvan forests. That's what I've been led to believe, yet my experience speaks differently. I visualize that my muse is a coarse, lumbering man, and judging by his humor, he is probably a foppish cross-dresser. I envision that Kevin Bruce pretends he has a Kewpie doll face, wears Sunday-school pumps, and puts grosgrain ribbons in his hair. I also imagine he's ham-fisted, clunk-footed, thick around the middle, incurably off-balance, and limited to about a thirty-degree range of motion in all his joints.

Typically I am pestered by Kevin Bruce's voice in my head, and he won't let me relax until I record his afflatus. I've heard that muses are tender creatures, cajoling their protégés into creativity with gentle inspiration. Not mine. He's more of the hag-ridden variety.

Kevin Bruce visits me with his dithyrambs at the most inconvenient times: when I'm showering, driving, falling asleep … drunk. No matter, for I dry off, pull over, wake up, sober up, and write diligently. I deserve credit for that.

Inconvenience notwithstanding, to have a muse is to be recognized, and I am respectful of that privilege. I'm fond of Kevin Bruce, sincerely. He's got a connection to me, but I can't explain it. Maybe my mom had an ovarian teratoma when I was an embryo and Kevin Bruce is my dermoid cyst. Kevin Bruce visits me with words that torment me until I get them out of my head and put them down in writing. That's probably why I drink so much. Kevin Bruce's voice sounds a lot sweeter to me when I've been drinking.

So there we have it: I'm constructing my therapeutic diary following the classical literary model of thanking my muse and starting in medias res. I could just write this diary as action without a plot, but like most tosspots, I have difficulty keeping things simple. I wonder what my therapist will say about all that.

Before I advance too far in my writing, I should communicate here the observation that I honestly believe I am designed to be an ordinary human being but am beset in a way that deviates me from my constellation of picket-fence living. My blueprint is to be cut out of the middle of the middle, and I am inherently a common man by nature, marked by neither tragedy nor cure. No matter what happens, I can't break through to a life of peaceful living; but equally, neither can I seem to fail. I yearn for the impunity of my destiny, but I cannot tolerate the satisficer pathways required to get there. No matter how much I achieve or how much money I earn, I feel like Martha in the kitchen, preferring mundane duties, and as in Martha's case, this would be a good thing, except that a global influence is in the living room of my life.

I guess that if we tell our stories honestly, and if we avoid hagiographic autobiography, and if we write without using the opportunity to belittle our enemies or make excuses for ourselves, then our story represents everyone's story. In that way, it's good to be the middle of the middle like me. If a diary can have a theme, then I hope that one will be mine—to represent a prevailing journey traveled by many.

CHAPTER 3

The Iliad, The Divine Comedy, and The Odyssey

Into the battering torment of two-way wind, the carnal sinners are thrust. These are the sinners who place their reason beneath the yoke of their lust … They speak, they hear, they're whirled down one and all … In tempest torn by warring winds, the stormy blast of Hell with restless fury drives the lustful onward, dashed!

—Dante Alighieri, from *The Divine Comedy*, "Inferno," cantos IV and V

Today I told Pat about my first knowledge of women. It's an interesting story. It's one of the first sessions where she listened to me at length without asking a lot of questions. I noticed the change in her rhythm. I also told her about Kevin Bruce. Come to think of it, that's just about when she got quiet. It might not be a coincidence.

The story is that two of my cousins and I were walking on railroad tracks through the Ohio woods one summer day. My cousins are my peers in age: one a year older, and the other a year younger. As would be the hallmark of my life, I was in the middle. I was nine years old at the time, so my elder cousin would have been something like ten, and my younger cousin about eight. We watched heat devils dance in the distance ahead of us and behind us on the tracks. They probably danced among us too, but heat devils can't be seen up close. No devils can.

I remember being thirsty. Odd how I should still feel that thirst in my throat when I have this memory after four decades, but I do. I literally feel it in my throat, particularly on the left side. I told Pat about it once.

"It's probably a side effect of your cholesterol medication," she said. Pat has a flippant way of deromanticizing my comments. She's Irish Catholic.

Life finds children, and it found us three boys that day, there on those railroad tracks. Elan disguises itself as an adventure and delivers itself as a milestone. Circumstance mixes with chance and coincidence, and a lesson results. One such occurrence was about to find us three boys.

Pow! There it hit us—a stack of girlie magazines! This was before the days of instant porn, so catching hold of naked women in print was indeed a treasure. Up to that point, the closest thing we'd experienced relating to women and sex came from television, where some kind of new pill had the country in an uproar and something called abortion was killing babies. "Damn Redstockings!" my father kept spouting around the house. I wasn't sure what the color of stockings had to do with anything, but I knew stockings were undergarments that went around women's legs up under their dresses and I shouldn't talk about anything in that neighborhood, so I didn't ask. I also knew to not interact with my father when he was in these moods. My mother remained quiet. I guess she was practicing self-preservation, like me, but it's hard to know what silence means.

The girlie magazines had been wrapped in a plastic bag and carefully placed under the floor of a workman's shed on the edge of the tracks. My cousins and I had seen the shed dozens of times, and we usually played around it as we frolicked by. The shed was locked this day, as usual, but that didn't matter, because we found our treasure under the building, not inside of it.

Stacks of cemented bricks supported the corners of the shed a foot or two up off the dirt. This is plenty of room for boys. These areas make great homes for reptiles and furry creatures, which is why we three boys made it a point to look under the shed whenever we were in the area. People who hide things in such places don't at all understand the workings of a boy's mind; otherwise, they would never, ever, conceal anything there. The magazines were clearly hidden by an adult.

"Look at this! Dirty magazines! Quick, bring them out!" The withdrawal of those magazines was our moment of pulling a sword from a rock. It was marvelous.

Within these magazines we would see something we never dreamed possible: the unclad bodies of women who showed themselves on purpose. We were amazed to see that these women were having so much fun even though somebody was taking naked pictures of them. We didn't know them, yet we were seeing them undressed! Our little world had gone upside-down.

These women contradicted everything I knew. They were strong, they were direct, and they were naked. They didn't slap me, make fun of me, or yell at me to leave. They didn't make me feel bad in any way. I wasn't accustomed to such kindness from girls. It was confusing.

"As I looked at the magazines, my eyes burned," I said to Pat as I told her about the memory. "I thought God was punishing me for seeing forbidden fruit."

"You probably just weren't blinking."

"Don't underestimate the power of that moment," I said to Pat, somewhat disdainfully. "My cousins and I speculated about the magazines being like those secret government files we had heard about—the ones that go up in smoke after you look at them. I checked my fingers for traceable dye. I literally looked at my fingertips."

"What were you three boys doing as you looked at the pictures? Were you masturbating?"

"No. Absolutely not. That was a subject we didn't ever discuss, so I don't know about the other two, but I was afraid my dick would fall off if I touched it. We just sat on the tracks, close to each other so we could look at not only the magazines balancing on our own bony knees, but also at the pictures the others were holding as well. We were in titty overload, and I was doing my best just to keep from fainting backward onto the tracks. I didn't hear a thing, and by the way, I wasn't thirsty anymore."

I described to Pat that I was sitting between my two cousins, directly in the middle. I described my amazement at the softness and beauty of the women in the pictures; I was absorbed by the desire they inspired, and dumbfounded at the sight of them. Their curves and lines sucked all my concentration.

After a while, we boys lost our muscle-tension dysphonia and were able to speak again. I don't remember who said what, and it doesn't matter, because we were all probably saying the same things.

"Look! She's got ninnies!"

"Right up front!"

"And she shows 'em!"

"On purpose!"

One of my cousins unfolded a three-page centerfold of a woman in gynecological repose, and we thought it was the most beautiful thing we had ever seen. Our heads jerked backward as the pages flipped open toward us. The woman in the centerfold was smiling.

"Just think. Every girl in school has ninnies." The words came out in exhausted puffs.

"No—they don't—can't!"

"You really think they might?"

"They have to."

"And these too?"

"Noooooooooo!"

"This one's touching herself down there. It looks like an oyster."

"Stop pretending you've ever seen an oyster."

"I have—in pictures! Look; here's another one!"

"You've never seen an oyster before."

"Have too!"

"Liar!"

"Shut up, both of you! Someone might hear."

"I wonder if all girls have this fuzz."

"The oyster looks wet."

"I think they spray it so it shines for the picture."

"They do! I heard about it."

"When I grow up, I want to be the guy who takes these pictures."

"I want to be the guy who sprays the oysters."

I won't ever know the women in those pictures, but I wouldn't be surprised if they wanted exactly the vista we three created. The respect. The instruction. The admiration.

Until now, I've told this story to only one other person—a woman, which somehow makes the telling even more poignant. We were lovers. We were both divorced. I was somewhere in my early thirties at the time, and she in her late forties. It strikes me as I write these words that I am a few years older now than she was then.

We were alone in her home after work, splayed on her bed enjoying a dreamy state of postcoital relaxation. Since we were alone, all the doors in the house were open, and we could hear the television playing evening news in her den down the hall. It was the early 1990s, and a thing called the internet was becoming available for unrestricted access to instantaneous, unfiltered information of all kinds. Television commentators were abuzz over what this might mean for humanity. Government leaders expressed concern about national security. Theologians dwelt on pornography.

It was this last part which reminded me of finding the treasure of magazines with my two cousins a quarter-century before that. My, how times had changed—even then.

I told the story to my lover slowly. She listened the entire time with her head on my shoulder while she softly played with the hair on my chest. My arm wrapped around her shoulders, and I absentmindedly fingertip-brushed her lower back and hips as I told her the details.

When I finished, she was silent. Thinking I had said too much, I asked what she was feeling. I braced myself, for I had learned through personal experience to fear my own questions to women.

After a pause, she responded. She barely moved a muscle while she spoke. Her words were wonderful.

She said there wasn't a woman alive who hadn't secretly fantasized in her quiet, sensual moments about what we three boys did. She said no warm-blooded woman on earth could ignore the tenderness of our sweet reaction with its clumsy innocence and awestruck admiration. She said she wished the right woman could have nurtured me, giving herself to me and bringing me rightly into my gentlemanhood, teaching me the art and skill of lovemaking, of when and where and how—and how much. She said she wished she could have whispered the answers to my softly asked questions and opened the closed doors of my uncertainty.

After telling her my story and hearing her response, the woman and I spent the rest of the evening and night in bed. We kissed and caressed each other long past sunset and deep into the night. We each had several more orgasms, yet for all the hours we spent in bed that night, we had intercourse only once, and that was before I told her my story. I explored her body as a boy would do it, full of looks and touches and kisses, but nothing more. I guess, through her, I was thanking the women in the pictures. It was as if they were all connected somehow, and in some mysterious and wonderful way, I was doing things to her that I wanted to do to them. For all I knew, she was one of the women in the pictures. She very well could have been. Even if she wasn't, she was.

As I look back across the eras of my life, I see women who helped me and men who did their jobs. Pity I blew past the first group and tried so hard to impress the second. I'm not making sweeping macrogender statements here, but I feel I should have done a better job of reciprocating to the specific women who helped me. I intend to amend that behavior every time I have the chance.

Relevant to telling Pat during that therapy session about the magazines and my ex-lover is that she handed me a tablet and a pen after I finished talking and asked me to make two lists: one list naming the worst people I knew personally and noting a few adjectives summarizing what they did to earn my disdain, and another list naming the best people I knew and a few adjectives describing what they did to earn my admiration. It took about five minutes, then I handed her the tablet.

"Did you notice that all the names on the list of people you admire are women?" she asked.

Too dumbfounded to reply when she said that, I just looked at her. "I take that as a no," she said.

I didn't set out to document any kind of gender reflection, but there was a meaningful pop-up correlation: the bad list was shared by men and women equally, but the good list was only women. The ascertainment struck me immediately. Karma has a laser beam.

"Which people do you think about more frequently—the people on the list of who you respect, or the people on the list of who you hold in disdain?"

I thought for a little while and then said, "Sadly, I often think about people who aggravate me, but I only occasionally remember people I value."

"That's common," she said, "so don't beat yourself up about it, but I want you to be aware of it and try to reverse that behavior. When you catch yourself rehearsing an event that angers you, make yourself deliberately think about the people who have had a positive effect on you. The reason is that we tend to absorb and internalize the people we think of most often, so if you think most often about the negative people in your life, you'll tend to emulate the group you don't respect." I valued her advice, but I also noticed she kept my list of names. She didn't usually do that with the things I handed her during our sessions.

I didn't know the name of a metaphor when I was a preadolescent boy sitting on those railroad tracks, looking at pictures of naked women; but I saw the women's strength, independence, and beauty as being more important than their nudity. To me it was emblematic as much as it was sexual. I was perspicacious but dewy-eyed even then, which is exactly the kind of combination Pat warned me against during our very first session. She still does.

Through those pictures, I had looked under the thin veil of women's clothing to see wondrous things. Using parallel analogy, I remember mulling what other things might be just beneath surface of what we see and think we know, including what we see and think we know about ourselves.

Sitting there that day between my two cousins on the railroad tracks, I eventually looked away from the magazines, and I gazed into the distance. The furthest reach of my vision down those tracks through the heat devils was opaque, almost translucent. I thought about what might be out there beyond my own well-worn pathways, and I made a commitment to try to find out. I've spent my life pursuing that commitment.

Now, decades later, I write these words in therapeutic reflection. I know us three boys not only then on the tracks, but also into our future, for I now know how our three lives have gone since then. We were *The Iliad* and *The Divine Comedy* and *The Odyssey*, elbow to elbow. If our parents had told each of us to bring home milk and bread after school and gave us a few dollars to pay for it, there's only one boy who could have actually succeeded at the errand, and it wasn't me. Of the remaining two, one would forget, and the other would get kicked out of school for gambling or buying contraband with the cash. I was the one who would forget.

Just before we left those railroad tracks, my cousins and I deliberated about what to do with the magazines. Suggestions ranged from "burn them now so we can hide the evidence" to "sneak them into our bedrooms." Ever the moderate, I suggested simply returning them to where we'd found them. After a debate, which I somehow won for a change, we decided to put them back in exactly the same place under the shed. No one would know the magazines had been disturbed, and the FBI wouldn't investigate the crime. We had seen pictures of naked women, so we thought it was best to play it cool. Criminals shouldn't attract attention after a heist. That's another thing we had learned from television.

We made an impromptu ceremony out of returning our treasure, and then retreated in soft-footed reverence as if we were backing away from royalty on a throne. For better or worse, we were what we were—born that way. As guided pathways go, hormones and upbringing make for some pretty strong railroad tracks. Paganism is a powerful thing.

My first experience with a real girl came six or eight years later. We didn't have sex exactly, but we were headed in that direction. She was my girlfriend, and I wanted to have sex with her, but I also wanted everyone in her family to know that I was honorable and that I would protect her and treat her with abstinence, which my elders coded in conversations as "respect." My sense of duty was stronger than my libido, which is odd for a teenager, so I did indeed "respect" her.

One Friday night, my girl and I went for a walk on a gravel road in the woods beside a creek. We were alone. We had been to the movies and watched *Shampoo*. It starred Warren Beatty. I had mixed feelings about him as an actor. We could hear the creek babbling not far away through the trees as we as we walked and talked about Warren Beatty. My girl liked him a lot, which probably contributed to my mixed feelings about him. In the movie, he had a lot of women, which I thought would offend her. It didn't, and I didn't like that it didn't. I remember that the creek sounded fresh and squeaky-clean.

As we walked, we came upon a rock jutting from the edge of the bank out into the flowing water. It was a big rock but not huge, just about car-sized. It was large enough for the two of us to sit on together, nestled privately among the trees and bushes. The setting was as picturesque as our mood was tender.

I sat behind my girlfriend on the rock. She was between my legs with her back against my chest. Her head rested on my shoulder. I wrapped my arms around her to keep her warm.

After a time of bolstering myself for the task, I slowly raised my right hand and touched her breast through her sweater. She shifted her posture a little. I didn't know if she was startled or aroused. My touch was gawky. In an attempt to be gentle, I substituted slowness for gracefulness. Constant attention and a bumbling kind of awkwardness are the surest indication of earnestness among suitors, and I had plenty of both.

I had not done anything like this before. I hadn't even tried. My girl put her hand on top of mine. I didn't squeeze her breast; I just kept my hand upon her. It was enough for me that it was there.

Her breasts were small. I began to explore them. I sometimes cupped her entire breast in the palm of my hand, and sometimes I touched her nipples slowly through her sweater with the very tips of my fingers. We were not speaking or kissing. My touch remained soft and thoughtful.

After a while, I put my hand inside her sweater. I fumbled with the buttons on her blouse, so she helped me, which I interpreted as a sign of love. She was adept where I was clumsy, which I took as a sign that she outclassed me.

I touched her bra. I was surprised at how thin and silky the material felt in my hand. Her nipples were pronounced.

I moved my fingertips under her bra. I couldn't believe my hands were now on her bare breasts! Directly on them! What an honor! I could feel her heart pounding under my fingertips. I was speechless. She validated her love for me by letting me do this to her. I was sure, because I knew that the only reason girls allow boys to touch their bodies is because of love. I knew that for a fact—but I didn't know why I knew it for a fact. I just knew.

She breathed deeply against me. If I had been more experienced, I would have recognized her invitation.

After a while, I repositioned her bra over her small breasts. I nimbly buttoned her blouse and removed my hands from under her sweater. I was amazed at how deft I had become in only that little while. I very softly pressed my cheek against her ear and whispered, "Thank you."

I closed my eyes, pressed my lips against her temples, and whispered an actual prayer of thanks to God for giving me this girl. I knew we would be happy forever. She had given me a perfect first experience, and I hoped I had done the same for her.

Darkness was descending upon our little cocoon, and along with the sun went the last rays of warmth. We emerged through the branches onto the gravel road and made our way back to the car. I valued her.

I started to think, and even though thinking might always be best, it isn't always advisable. Sometimes we're better off just sitting on rocks in the woods and leaving it at that.

"Are you a virgin?" I blurted.

I don't know where the words came from. I had not really considered the question before asking it, for I had not yet been trained by life to fear my own questions. The thought popped out of my lips without hesitation because I was absolutely sure of the answer. I thought I knew all there was to know. There is no reason to use caution if we think there is no danger.

My girlfriend was quiet for a while, but I didn't initially notice. I was too caught up in my own bliss.

"Why did you ask me that?" she eventually replied. This wasn't the response I expected. I wasn't sure why, but I didn't like it. The person asking questions is the one who takes control, and here she was asking a question. It wasn't like her to ask questions. Her rhythm had shifted to a new beat, and even in my clueless youth, I recognized that as a bad sign.

"I'm sorry," I softly said. "I didn't mean to be rude. I guess I was just wondering out loud. Please don't be mad."

"It's okay," she reassured me before slipping into quietness. Her silence screamed, and I felt guilty for tarnishing our magic moment.

Soon I started thinking different thoughts, and my reaction turned from guilt to uneasiness. She had taken charge of the conversation, and I felt a little as though she had done it by design.

I'd had heard tales from my schoolmates and my father. They were stories about girls, and they weren't kind. They used words like "leftovers." The stories were all about things boys had done to girls and about all the things girls gave boys that they couldn't take back and about how stupid the girls were for doing it and how the girls made fools of themselves because of love for the boys.

Worse than the talk of the girls was the talk of their future boyfriends and what suckers those poor bastards would be, as if the new boyfriend could only be an afterthought second-stringer for the rest of his life. Second string forever is a weighty verdict to carry on behalf of someone else's sins. It was a terrible situation. I didn't want my girl to be the girl they were talking about, and I damn sure didn't want to be the condemned second-string boyfriend. I wanted to be exempt from that entire state of affairs. All she had to do was be a virgin. It was just that simple!

"Are you …?" I asked again with some caution. The words came out of my mouth hesitantly this time. Only a few minutes earlier, I owned the world. The bluntness of my inexperience had now been replaced by the hesitation of my fear.

She responded to my question with yet another question, and I didn't like it one bit. "Would it make any difference?" she asked.

Without even doing it on purpose, I did a very adult thing: I skirted the issue. It was a sad and mature talent to acquire.

"The important thing is that you know you can talk to me," I said to her. It sounded like the kind of answer that a cool, modern, sensitive, confident man of the 1970s should give, so I gave it. Like most acts of compromise, it was successful but not pleasing. In the long run, pretense is never a good substitute for authenticity. One can sweep only so much fraudulence under the sad rug of reality before tripping over the mound.

"You know you can trust me," she finally said.

I noticed she herself was skirting the issue. She sounded just like me only a moment earlier. I tensed. Why wouldn't she just answer my question? A watched pot never boils. I guess she sensed my uneasiness, because she finally answered my question with a direct answer.

"Yes, I'm a virgin," she said.

It would not have been an overstatement to say that the earth stopped quaking and the sky opened and the heavens rejoiced. Evil had been thwarted, and a burden of biblical proportions lifted from me. My world once again enjoyed a nice, smooth spin. I thought that God and the girl must have been testing me, and I hoped I had performed well.

"Actually, I lied," she faintly murmured. The words struggled out of her throat as if she were impelling them by an act of will, and though they were barely audible, their impact more than compensated for their softness.

Once she hit me with the big news, the details must have seemed easy, because they poured out of her. This girl who could not speak became the woman who would not shut up. When a newly freed pendulum launches, it slings to the farthest reaches of its previously pent-up energy. She was relieving herself of a long-restrained vehemence and giving it to me with all the strength it previously took to contain it.

"My first boyfriend was my next-door neighbor on Paris Boulevard," she said. "I was thirteen. Jason was his name. I loved him with all my heart …"

She kept talking. I remember every word, and I remember even more veraciously how they made me feel. All these years later, those words still echo in my mind as if she said them to me just a little while ago. She told me about Jason having sex with her when she was thirteen and how she loved him beyond all else. I felt sick to my stomach when she told me about becoming the school tramp to get revenge against Jason. She thought he would miss her more if he was jealous about her having sex with all the other boys in school. Then came the worst part.

"Once, I was in the back of my garage with one of the boys, and my Uncle Paulo caught us having sex. The boy was doing it to me on the hood of my dad's car, so I was bent under him, and I didn't know my uncle was there. He saw everything. He told the guy to leave and never come back. The boy couldn't get out of there fast enough. I never felt so alone." She paused briefly and then continued. "I thought I was in big trouble when Uncle Paulo caught us, but then he said he wouldn't tell anyone as long as I had sex with him, so I did it. I didn't like it, but I did it. After that I had to keep doing it so he would keep staying quiet. I got used to it. It's been going on a long time. I didn't say anything to anyone at first, because I was afraid and confused, but now I'm worried that if I talk, people might wonder what took me so long to say something. They might think I liked it. Maybe I do." The girl looked at me. "I know what you're thinking," she said, "but don't worry; he's only my aunt's husband, so he's not actually my uncle."

"Stupid bitch, you don't know what I'm thinking at all!" I wanted to scream these words, but I did not say them. In fact, I did not feel that I could speak at all, for only minutes earlier I had painted myself into a corner by luring her with false assurances that she could feel safe talking to me about anything. I wasn't exactly lying to her when I gave her that pledge, because I made it with an amateur's overconfidence that I could indeed shoulder the magnitude of anything that was to come. I had no clue.

I remained quiet as my girlfriend was talking, and I stayed that way for a long, long, long time afterward. I didn't realize it, but my relationship walls fortified quite a lot because of that pain, and I opened the gates only for women who appeared to be unblemished and guileless. Odd how it all seems so clear here on these pages, regarding not only what I did at the time of our breakup but also what I did in my relationships for years and years thereafter.

A shallow mind would say we were just a couple of hormonal teenagers overpowered by our emotions. A concerned observer might even add that our culture and upbringing left us unprepared. But a serious thinker would ask what put those powerful desires and expectations inside of us in the first place. Something ancient and preeminent must have considered desire and expectation to be very important, and then, dreadfully, something sordid vitiated those things afterward.

Following our breakup, I went with as many lovers as I could find—exactly as my girlfriend had done to mend her own broken heart before I met her. For my girlfriend and me both, this behavior was an amateurish attempt at emotional variolation.

I did as many things as I could to as many girls as would let me do those things to them. My only saving grace is that I did not ever force or pressure a girl into anything. Other than that, I was looking for more.

My sense of injury did not improve, and in fact, it sometimes even worsened. Solutions involving sex and romance tend to create more problems than they solve. Contrary to what injured people think, sexual eye-for-eye justice is neither lasting nor satisfying, and revenge will always be a poor substitute for healing. As it turns out, I wasn't morally superior after all. I was just uninfected.

CHAPTER 4

Kairos Timeline and Taste Berry Miraculin

Among the bitter sloes, it befits not the sweet fig tree to bear fruit.
These are an avaricious, envious, and proud folk, hostile to thee
because of thy good deeds; covetous since times remote. From their
customs take heed to cleanse thyself, lest thou be polluted.
Dante Alighieri, from *The Divine Comedy*, "Inferno," canto I

I graduated from high school in 1976. I was seventeen years old. A year or so later, I joined the US Army for a three-year enlistment. I was a patriotic kid ready to fight, kill, and die because I believed it was my duty; but make no mistake—when my enlistment was over, it was over. I had seen my duty and done it.

I went home. I would like to report that it was a joyous homecoming and I received a hero's welcome, but the truth is that as soon as I went back, I realized why I had left in the first place. I was exceedingly disappointed, and it's a relevant part of my therapy to document the enormity of that huge fact. The shitty leadership in my shitty town resulted in a collapsed economy, and I returned to a tumbleweed memorial. The only thing on the rise around those parts was the crime rate. Knowing myself to be too hip for the house, I left for good a few months later.

Roots never grow back after something like that happens to a young person. As if my local experience wasn't bad enough, the entire nation didn't give a shit about military veterans in the 1970s. Those were tough years to serve in the military. Jimmy Carter was president. Under his administration, the country invested in higher education.

Joining the army was the best thing I did as a young person. It removed me from my bad-influence relationships at home and exposed me to new and better ways of daily living. I mean that with absolutely no sarcasm. As it turned out, I wasn't from a gene pool of people who are inherently toothless, penniless, and stinky; we just didn't know about dental hygiene, asset preservation, or how to keep aerobic bacteria from growing in our clothing. Since my flaws weren't hereditary, when I applied myself, I could rise above them. There's a thing called "cultural literacy," and that's all I was lacking. By this measure, the army taught me how to read.

That's the good part. The bad part is that the young, disruptive activist protesters of the 1960s were achieving positions of leadership by the late 1970s, and America was morphing from a duty-driven society into a complaint-driven society. I was ill equipped for America's newly adopted squeaky-wheels-get-the-grease ideology. My lot in life seems to be that of a mechanic with a grease gun.

I think regularly about something that happened to me during my travel home. It epitomizes much.

At the airport just outside of my military post, I met a man who had been booted out of the army for being more trouble than he was worth. Nessus Pholus was his name. It's an odd name, so it stuck in my mind. It's also an irritating name, so it had a kind of onomatopoetic parallel with his annoying personality.

I had been a civilian for only a few hours when I first met Pholus, and I was basking in my new-veteran status, waiting at the airport for my flight home. I was twenty-one years old, and my whole life was ahead of me. Things looked bright. As Pat often points out, I was setting myself up for disappointment. As usual, she's right.

I was a veteran with an honorable discharge, and I was seriously proud of it! I should put more exclamation points behind that statement, because I can't understate my feeling of having finished something good. I was a veteran, and I was proud! All I wanted was to sit quietly in my booth at the airport bar, sip on my drink, and reflect upon my accomplishment.

"What are you doing here?" Pholus asked me, bluntly. The question came so unexpectedly that it startled me.

"Waiting for my flight," I replied, somewhat bewildered.

Looking back from the perspective of my now-thickened skin, I don't even know why I gave Pholus an answer. Lucky for him I was still a polite young person at that time. I had yet to kill anyone and was more inclined to mollify than to exterminate. These days, that clown wouldn't have gotten out of the airport alive. My, my, my—how I have changed.

"Any chance you could just leave me alone?" Pholus asked.

"Okay," I said, and I immediately turned my face away from him. He hovered for a moment and then sat with me in my booth. I looked at him across the table in indignant amazement, but I remained quiet. It bears repeating that I have changed.

I still had my 1950s-era army-regulation coiffure, and I guess Pholus saw it at the airport and knew I was military. He had a haircut just like mine. I guessed Pholus was fresh out, like me; but unlike me, he didn't seem proud.

Pholus told me the military hadn't done anything for him. I was offended by his words because I had enlisted to serve, and even die if I had to, but he had enlisted to get benefits. Few things are more offensive to a veteran than a scaramouch with an honorable discharge.

Pholus talked, and then he talked some more. For variety, he said things. And when he was done orating, he blathered. As bad as that was, he had only two categories of conversation: how he made fools of people, and how his rights had been violated. He had a knack for both criticizing and complaining in the very same sentence. He also smoked like a chimney. I thought it was ironic that he railed about global imperfections but then filled his lungs with carcinogens. He seriously needed to study the Serenity Prayer.

Other than Pholus's obvious mental illness and inability to stop talking, I remember his small hands. His arms decreased in size from his shoulders to his fingertips the same way a tree limb shrinks gradually into twigs. By contrast, I noticed my arms and hands were made of distinct stops, and each joint started with a thick-boned, muscle-cut new part. My hands were massive compared to his.

Pholus told me he had taken a discharge code V to get out of the army, and I knew exactly what it meant, because soldiers always joke about applying for one as a fruit-loop ticket home. "Celestine V" is what we called it, mockingly. Pholus described his discharge as a scheme he designed and orchestrated to outsmart the system because he realized the army was stupid and he had strategically chosen to end his enlistment. He referred to the mental instability code they gave him as a triviality—nothing more than a mere numerical designation to tell drone-like clerks exactly where they should put his paperwork in a huge warehouse filled with metal filing cabinets.

He told me with a snicker on his face that my papers would go into that same warehouse, and there our files would turn yellow together at the same rate in the same place nobody cared about. He told me our discharges were both honorable, but his was better because he was eligible for federal health care benefits that my discharge didn't include. Sadly for me, he was telling the truth about that. Everything about Nessus Pholus was a giant middle finger to me and the country I served, yet his benefits were better than mine.

I was thankful as our flights soon arrived and we boarded toward our separate destinies. It was deus ex machina for me, but I pity the poor souls in the seats near Pholus on his aircraft. With a little luck, maybe he married well and kept from starving to death. Lots of condescending, dysfunctional people do it. A lot of them have an honorable discharge code V.

Speaking of life-altering choices, it's time for me to include my marriage in this diary. The sequence is that after the army, I enrolled in college in New Orleans—all the way across the country from my family. Attending college here is what brought me to this city.

I met my ex-wife in college. I was a hard worker and a dedicated student, so I finished in three years. I started when I was twenty-one, and I graduated when I was twenty-four. It was the early 1980s. Those were tough years to pay for college. Ronald Regan was president. Under his administration, the country invested in military personnel.

My ex and I celebrated commencement together in May, and we married in June. She was a Yat, so we stayed in New Orleans to live with her family after college. In point of fact, her Yat accent is what made me notice her in college. When I first heard her talking in the cafeteria, I thought she was from Brooklyn. Being the lonely, displaced Yankee that I was, I struck up a conversation thinking I had found a fellow traveler. As was true throughout our marriage, I was terribly mistaken. My ex-wife is not a traveler of any kind, but the misunderstanding was my fault, not hers. She didn't ask me to assume we would journey together, or even that she wanted to go anywhere in the first place.

Residential living in a studious college environment is a valuable and desirable way to learn, but since it's so scripted, it doesn't bring out our genuine daily inclinations. Since my fiancée and I broke bread together and had a shared academic curriculum with matching deadlines, we thought we had a lot in common. We didn't, so real life hit us hard after the wedding.

Since I was a military veteran by the time I enrolled in college, and since I was several years older than most of my classmates, including my ex-wife, I thought I knew some things. Other boys were vulnerable to pretty faces and big boobs, and I very much enjoyed those things, but I wasn't looking for that in a life partner. I was a damaged Prince Charming on the hunt for a virginal Cinderella. I found one, and I married her.

She was my kryptonite—a fragile, vulnerable, hymeneal girl with a never-ending smile on her lips and a constant expression of concern in her eyes. She always looked cold. Skinny people usually do.

Heterosexual young men who are as pompous and overblown as I was will always be attracted to brides like my ex. I thought I was ready to settle down, and the timing seemed right, so in addition to feeling as if I had finally found someone who deserved me, she was someone I thought I could rescue. I thought she needed assistance and protection, and since I felt she had earned her top-drawer marriageability through a lifestyle of abstinence and chastity, I recompensed her by offering myself as her reward. She was a lousy lover, but I believed I could tutor her conjugal skills as time passed. Unfortunately for me, what I interpreted as virginity based on morality, virtuousness, and self-discipline was really just disinterest in men on all three counts. One should be careful what one asks for.

My ex-wife is a nice person, and my documentation of our marriage will not be complete without including that statement. I mean it boldly and literally; she's a nice person. She's a good citizen, a devoted employee, an honor-bound daughter, a courteous driver, and an active church parishioner. Those are all very good things, and I mean that statement with no artifice. These are very good things indeed, and she is every one of them in abundance. If you're picking members of your community, then you should pick people who are exactly like my ex-wife—but be forewarned: the divorce rate is going to be monstrously high, because nowhere on that list did I mention "great spouse."

All these things I've written about my ex-wife are accurate; however, in the spirit of therapeutic diaries, I need to be sure to communicate a balanced picture. The nebulous truth is that I let her down.

I've matured in many ways since my marriage. For one, I learned that the way in which we enter a situation tends to define our roles for as long as we remain within that situation, and since I entered my marriage as its doyen, I had no right to turn around later and criticize my wife for not being much of a coequal. It wasn't false advertising on my part to act as if I had everything under control at the time of our vows; I was just a hollow young person playing a role. As it turned out, so was she.

Sadly, this was not the first time I had made the mistake of promising support to a woman in ways I could not deliver. I should have known better.

There's one last thing I need to write about my ex-wife as an item of relevance to my psychological state of mind: she's a lesbian submissive. I didn't know it at the time, and I didn't learn it until years after our divorce, but looking back, it explains a hell of a lot.

In fairness to my ex-wife, I'm not accusing her of lying to me about her sexual preferences, because she probably didn't know the truth about herself—not at first anyway. I suspect that, true to form for lesbian submissives, she wasn't capable of knowing she was a lesbian submissive until someone told her that's what she is. Pat is helping me recognize and recover from that damage.

That said, I've learned to be careful about launching arrows of justice at people, because my bow shoots backward quite a lot—usually when I least expect it. Communicating about my ex-wife is a good example. Kevin Bruce has clued me into realizing that what I didn't know about her is really a reflection of what I didn't know about myself, so I need to be patient and forgiving of her and myself with equal generosity. Pouters like me tend to complain a lot that we didn't deserve what happened to us, but Pat and Kevin Bruce have both cautioned me not to base my interpretations on what I really deserve. Life isn't fair, and I benefit from that fact every day.

So that was my marriage. We didn't have any children or debts, and after signing some papers, we slid out from each other's lives. That was that. Mr. and Mrs. Docile were done. I had a girlfriend by the end, and as it turns out, so did my ex-wife. Making lemonade out of lemons, I can report that we finally have something in common: we each left our marriage for big-busted, bossy women, and neither relationship lasted.

One good thing came out of the years I spent married. My ex-wife's family was wealthy, and being among them augmented my understanding of the real impact of money. It's powerful, but it complicates things, particularly when it lands upon us all at once, as happens when we marry into it. Marrying into wealth looks a lot better from the curb than from inside the house.

Years later, I made a fortune investing in opportunities to take windfall money from poor people who suddenly found themselves with economic leverage. Through my abrupt involvement with my in-laws' lavish lifestyle, I learned that a tidal wave of opulence sweeps us away, makes us forget who we are, and inspires us to make compromised decisions. Even though their money wasn't mine and they never let me forget it, I very definitely changed for the worse within that plentitude, and I also very definitely made myself remember the lessons I learned so that I could cash in on nouveau riche people in the future. The less they did to earn the money they had, the easier it was for me to take it away.

Speaking of education, I graduated with a bachelor's degree just before my wedding. During my marriage, I earned my master's degree. Around the time of our separation and divorce, I started a PhD at Louisiana State University. A few years later, after graduating with the PhD, I went on to earn a law degree. Void of fulfillment in one area, I guess I searched for satisfaction in another. Choosing healthy outlets for my unspent get-up-and-go, I was the most studious man on the planet during those years. We all have our ways of self-medicating, and mine was to earn credentials in the hopes that they would lead to a brighter future.

I was in my early thirties when I lost my desire to take any more classes. It seemed to vanish overnight, and suddenly I just couldn't go to college anymore. Up until then, I was still selecting traditional pathways to education, but I changed. That's when I really began to learn.

CHAPTER 5

Zeebo, Orphaned Eldest Son of Calpurnia

Let us descend below. We must go down. Look how thou enter here; beware in whom thou place thy trust. Let not this wide entrance deceive thee to thy harm.

THROUGH ME THE ROAD TO THE CITY OF DESOLATION
THROUGH ME THE ROAD TO SORROWS DIUTURNAL
THROUGH ME THE ROAD AMONG LOST CREATIONS

JUSTICE MOVED MY GREAT MAKER
GOD ETERNAL WROUGHT ME
POWER AND UNSEARCHABLY HIGH WISDOM
PRIMAL LOVE SUPERNATURAL

NOHING ERE I WAS MADE WAS MADE TO BE, SAVE THINGS ETERNAL
AND I ETERNAL ENDURE

ABANDON ALL HOPE, YE WHO ENTER HERE

—Dante Alighieri, from *The Divine Comedy*, "Inferno," canto III

Soon after my divorce, I met a new friend. I think I was thirty-two years old at the time, but maybe not quite. His name is Obra, and he comes from one of those big-money New Orleans families that secretly run things but never seem to be in the news.

Big-money families tend to adopt strays, and I was ripe for the picking. Low-class people huddle together in their neophobic households and snarl at outsiders, but high-class people reach out for new investments, including relationships. Somewhere in that period, I found myself holding keys to half the mansions in town. Obra is the best friend I've ever had. Pat has a lot to ask about Obra and my relationship with him, but Kevin Bruce never mentions him at all. Not ever.

Obra looks like a smaller version of Alan Alda. In fact, that's one of my nicknames for him: Alan. He also looks a little like Dr. Oz, so sometimes I call him Alan Oz. We give many names to the things we love.

Obra's family is right about a lot of things, and relationship management is high on the list of their wisdom. Early in my career, I kept looking for better jobs, but what I should have been looking for are better people. Better relationships with better people result in a better life. Without improving our relationships, nothing ever gets better. We can handle that reality in one of two ways: either fix the people we have or get new people. Whichever way we go, the statement bears repeating: without improving our relationships, nothing ever gets better.

I remember from my college studies learning about the major states of life and the crisis transitions we experience as we cross from one phase to another. The first phase is sexual, and I had already passed over that threshold. The next phase is career identity, and I was reaching for that doorknob.

I was a public schoolteacher when my career first started. I was in my midtwenties, a military veteran, a recent college graduate, and a newlywed. I was attentive to all those things, but only in superficial ways. Most of my attention went to my ego. I was an inch deep and a mile wide.

As far as my job is concerned, I achieved the ass-kisser's version of success, but nothing more. Ass kissing is the second-string portraiture of virtue signaling, and I practiced it a lot. It backfired.

Eventually I left the classroom and started working at the central office in the school system. I thought it was a promotion. It wasn't.

Above the main entrance to the school system offices is an inscription that says, "Welcome to the Florentine Parish School District, where hopes become reality!" That's not what it should have said. It should have said the opposite, something like "You have a quick and agile mind, but you should dumb that down a little."

I exceeded the paper requirements for my promotion, but the truth is my credentials had nothing to do with the approval of my application. I was a good enough errand boy and overall Frisbee chaser to get hired, but that about sums up what my supervisors cared about. At the time, I believed my new job was a reward for the high quality of my work, but I was a fool. That's the way I was up until I met Obra and he started to mentor me. I've come to be more realistic about myself since then.

Unfortunately, cachet is a false god, yet I yearned for it. Since I was defined by my résumé almost as much as by the sexual portraiture of my partners, success at work was extremely important to me. I can't overemphasize that point. In my mind, everything came a distant third to life partners and job titles. Not long after I met Obra, I knew I had failed at those two things horribly.

I cannot overdocument here in this diary how foolish I will always feel for being loyal to the people who hired me into the central office. They brought me on board to suit their needs, not mine. It's true that I owed them an honest day's work for an honest day's pay, but I did not owe them the subservience I offered up as lagniappe. They hired me to run errands and take blame, nothing more.

After he learned my story, Obra said my approach to achievement was flawed: I was trying to take the safe path up the mountain of success by being good and earning credentials. Obra advised I should get to my goals by traveling a longer, lower way and by being useful in concrete, measurable ways today, not in general. Abstract possibilities for the distant future are of little interest to predominant people.

Obra said I needed to get inside circles of power rather than knock on the door as a well-credentialed outsider. On the inside, we can gain leverage and be purposive. It's called influence. It's being involved in other people's angst and transporting them from their problems to their solutions—and debiting them for the passage. Obra was right.

Obra said I made a mistake by being associated only with goodness. He says it's a symptom of caring what other people think and that I need to stop letting other people's disapproval be my defining characteristic.

"Goodness is a public display at a crowded celebration," he told me. "It has no leverage, because it is its own reward. That stage is already full, and the participants don't want any new shareholders. If you want to be truly valuable, then you have to be in a position to help people when they're alone and in trouble. You're willing to do dirty work, and it shows, but you're doing the kind of dirty work that only results in approval, nothing more."

Obra and I are both fans of classic film, and we use them as metaphors constantly. "You think of yourself as Atticus Finch, but you're really Zeebo. Atticus Finch looks like a hero by shooting a rabid dog while everyone is afraid and watching. Then he leaves, yet the rabid dog is still there. He didn't remove it at all; he just put on a show. Nobody sees Zeebo, the garbage collector who actually removes the still-dangerous dog, making the neighborhood clean and safe again. Stop being Zeebo. He didn't even get to appear in the film, and his mother spent all her time taking care of other children."

Big-money families are usually involved in education, so it's no coincidence that my friendship with Obra blossomed when I went to work in the central office. Their motivation is part social and part business, so I suspect that at first, Obra's interest in our friendship was mostly financial. As a card-carrying member of the big-money crowd, Obra visited the system offices quite a bit.

If not for Obra's tutelage, I would have developed a pointlessly bad attitude during those years because I came to equate authority with betrayal, and I grew to see the public as an ignorant, gluttonous beast. Obra encouraged me to see things much less emotionally and much more opportunistically. "If you want to be happy, work with people and think about things. You do it the other way around. That's why you're so sullen most of the time."

"Don't try to fix anything," he said often. "Just show up every day and work. Keep it simple like that. Stop judging people's flaws according to a standard of perfection, and stop maintaining an idealized vision of the way things should be; just accept what is and then ask yourself what's best for you in that circumstance. Tomorrow, take another look around and ask yourself the same question again. Then again the day after that. And after that."

There's one specific event that comes to my mind when I think about Obra and the school system. I had worked at the central office for a couple of years when I joined senior leadership on a weekend boat ride. Obra had organized the trip. The event signposts a significant turning point for me, so as silly as it initially sounds, that boat ride was serendipitous enough to deserve lengthy mention here in my diary because I crossed a kind of no-return threshold during that passage. The hardest part of any journey is leaving home, even if the journey is psychological, and getting on that boat was my metacognitive version of leaving home.

As one of their investments, Obra's family owns a major distributorship of instructional, data-storage, and communication supplies that spans all of greater New Orleans and the surrounding parishes. Quite a lot of their business came from selling books in the old days, and since then the family has added to their interests things like electronics and educational software marketed to school systems, library chains, hospitals, and other places like that. Obra's family maintains very close ties with their clientele, and they frequently organize planning sessions and retreats that last several days. This boat ride was one of those undertakings.

During these retreats, buyers can review options that best suit their public service needs. They can bond with the sales process in a relaxing, sedulous environment. They can also bond with each other. They bond with many things, people, and products alike. Obra provides all the necessary resin for that bonding to occur.

A funny thing about resin: it starts out soft and squishy, and it feels comfortable in that state—all gooey and embracing. It enfolds us like a form-fitting cushion, lava-flowing its glacial way into our every nook and cranny. But imperceptibly, the resin begins to thicken. It gets sticky, holding us in, and soon it's as hard as stone, permanently encapsulating everything it encased during the curing process. The aforementioned nooks and crannies create its greatest stronghold. The people on the boat with us had a lot of nooks and crannies.

Most of the board members and high-up muckety-mucks of my entire school system were on that boat. There was trouble on board, and Obra was studying it.

"If you pay attention, what you see people not doing can be as informative as what you see them doing," Obra said. The advice stayed with me. "The next time you're at a social event, pay attention to which women aren't drinking alcohol, and then get ready for the baby announcement," he joked. "And if the event turns out to be relevant in the future, look at pictures taken there and make a mental note of, first, who isn't in them at all, and second, who isn't in the same pictures together with the pregnant women."

People on that boat didn't want me aboard. I wasn't like them, I wasn't with them, and I wasn't one of them. I've heard it said that we should practice our accusations in front of a mirror before we speak, and that recommendation would have been good for the people on that boat, for their objections to me were telltale in many ways. They had much to hide—many nooks and crannies.

Imagine the irony of those high-ranking people revealing to Obra that they were worried about me: it's like coyotes telling a wolf that a collie might be dangerous. Obra was harvesting mountains of information, and for a change, so was I.

The captain of the boat was especially obstinate about not wanting me on board with the others. That surprised me because I thought he should just pilot the boat and quietly follow orders. Charon is his name. It's Cajun, and I remember it well because it has a distinctly seaworthy sound.

Obra told Charon and the others I was safe, so eventually they shrugged off their concerns. Isn't it ironic that apathy is the gateway to doom? A ride to the gallows in a limousine may be a ride in a limousine, but it's still a ride to the gallows. It turned out these people didn't really care about me after all.

It takes a trained mind to know the difference between prestidigitation and sorcery. Obra has that ability and knows how to use it; the vacant souls on Charon's boat did not.

We were on Acheron Bay. You can go there if you like. It's easy. Just go into the bowels of New Orleans, turn left in Caina Village, and the next thing you know, you're crossing Acheron Bay.

CHAPTER 6

Jeptha's Daughter

They seem so eager to pass over and be gone. Heaven's justice goads them on so that what should be their fear is now turned into desire …

I am left in distress, and I remain in suspense. "Yes" and "No" contend within my head, and do within my doubtful mind contest. As one who wills and then unwills his will, my thoughts remain at war between "I will" and "I will not."
—Dante Alighieri, from *The Divine Comedy*, "Inferno," cantos III and VIII

Suicide is an ironic concept because the thought of ending one's life never occurs to the asshats who should do it, while sadly, most of the people who kill themselves are among the few humans who deserve to live long, happy, comfortable lives. I planned my own suicide once. I guess I would have been in my late twenties at the time and beginning to sense the futility of my relationships and the vanity of my work. Those two things are the media through which I define myself, and when they turn sour, I feel that I have failed. I'm still that way a little, but I was very much that way as a young man. That's a mistake, because most of what people do is because of them and has little or nothing to do with us. This is a true and accurate observation, and it includes our loved ones as well as our coworkers and bosses. Good person that I was back in those days, I blamed myself for my rotten circumstances. I don't do that so much anymore. I guess I've become an asshat.

My suicide was designed to put me to rest in a way I found to be appropriate. Identifying what we want in our own death tells a lot about us. I wanted mine to be painless for me and free of bother for everyone else.

I was going to fill my wooden pirogue with concrete blocks and chains, and then I was going to row it out into one of the swamps around New Orleans. I would pull the boat through a pathless wood and across the abominable sand, and shove off from a pier. I even had the location identified—the Pier delle Vigne. It's just outside of the city. It's a hauntingly beautiful place.

I designed a note so nobody would wonder what happened, but I wouldn't tell anyone where my body could be found. I was going to chain the concrete blocks—and myself—to the pirogue and then shoot the hull full of holes. I would save the last bullet for my brain. The little boat and its cargo would drop into the water and out of the human race. That would be that. Except for the note explaining what I had done, there would be no trace of the deed.

I was still married at the time, but our marriage was appearing to fail. That is the saddest phase of divorce. People who've never been through a divorce think moving out and signing papers are the worst events, but they're not. By then you're busy with a lot of details, and the end has been clear for a long time. The saddest part of a dying marriage is earlier, when you still try to carry on with business as usual but the weight of a dead body dragging behind is getting heavier and heavier. You remember joy, but those feelings are in poor health.

I was also having trouble at work during that phase, not so much because it wasn't going well as because I wasn't feeling satisfied with its purpose. On the list of my flaws is that I'm extrinsically motivated, so when I lose faith in my purpose, I lose my primum mobile. Those were tough days.

I was really going to kill myself. I was really going to do it. Up until that point in my life, I was afraid to die, but not then—and, for the record, not so much after that either. We can be afraid of living without being afraid of dying.

Thoughts of murdering oneself open the door to concepts of murder in general, so I guess the time has come for me to retrace the process of my first homicide. It's embarrassing—not because of what I did, but because of the stumblebum way I eroded into manslaughter.

Obra was in a pissy mood on the particular Saturday my first murder began because I had just told him I was going to drop out of our yoga class. I was a man made of ox bones in a room full of scrawny women who could *ardha uttanasana* their foreheads onto their toenails without even straining, so can you blame me for switching back to boxing and weightlifting? I just wasn't any good at yoga. I could do *chaturanga dandasana* because of its similarity to push-ups, but I was bad at every other position and activity.

I was also weary of constantly having to reassure my classmates that I was there to exercise and not to leer at them in their skin-tight clothes while their bony asses were thrust up into the air. They glared at me as if I were a fisherman at a *fangsheng*. Based on their accusation-laced questions thinly veiled as conversation, I don't think they approved of my being in my early thirties and childless. *Sleepless in Seattle* was playing in movie theaters, and I think that was the yardstick used to measure my shortcomings. A guy can take only so much stink-eyed rebuke before he simply has to depart.

These women weren't even my type. Leaning against the walls of the lobby while waiting for class to begin, they all looked like mops propped there to dry. They were nothing but bones and blond hair—every one of them. Even Kevin Bruce speaks of these women with unconcealed disdain in his voice.

I told Pat about all this during one of our sessions. She was proud of the way I kept these women in perspective and outside of my head. It was a revelation to me when I realized I had made some progress. They didn't like me, and I didn't care. They are what they are, and I am what I am.

Obra and I ate at a drive-up for lunch that Saturday after yoga, and the people parked in the stalls around us had bad carhop etiquette. It made Obra's downcast mood even worse. For comic relief, an old man strolled past our front bumper walking a potbelly pig on a leash.

"I want to buy a Harley and ride it to Sturgis for bike week so I can see a bunch of biker babes who aren't afraid to show me their zoomers," I said. It seemed like perfect timing to say something outrageous like this to Obra while the pig was still in sight, so I said it without a hint of warning. Obra sat very literally slack-jawed in the car. Irony is the basis of our friendship, and sarcasm the foundation of our communication. My plan to razz him into happiness had worked before, so I was giving it a try.

Obra always alleged that I overvalued breasts, so in retribution, I frequently spiced our conversation with titty-bomb references just to yank his chain. It didn't matter that the references were contextually irrelevant; it only mattered that he felt pestered. He was too conservative to talk about breasts in a playful way, probably as a result of all that upper-crust, classical education he received as a child. I, however, have way too much trailer-park DNA in my veins to be burdened by the delicacies of subtlety, so I have absolutely no problem making impish references to a woman's snuggle-pups.

"What?!" Obra eventually spouted after I made the bike-week-and-zoomers comment. "Even if you can get to Sturgis on a motorcycle, which is doubtful, what makes you think women there would show you their breasts? It's more likely they would kick your ass."

"They're going to do it because I'm going to get a T-shirt telling them to do it; that's why." Obra was visibly stricken, so I continued. "On the front, it'll say, 'Show me your tits!' and on the back it'll say, 'Climb on, shut up, and press your boobies here!'" I looked at Obra with that big, goofy grin on my face I get when I feel I've never been cleverer. He cast me a sideways evil eye. The only thing more reprimanding than a sideways evil eye is an applause of slow, sarcastic clapping, which is another thing we frequently did to each other.

We didn't talk about Sturgis bike week again until we were back at my condo. Obra brought it up abruptly, so I knew it had remained on his mind from the carhop.

"Where is Sturgis anyway? Isn't it in Nebraska or something like that? That's a thousand miles away. You won't get out of Louisiana before your saddle sores force you to pull over. You'd better start your Kegel exercises now. Maybe that'll help you get tough … down there."

"South Dakota," I said over my shoulder as I was walking across the room to check my answering machine. I kept one on top of my television as part of the focal point of my den.

The quality of my life in those days could be measured by encrypted telephone messages like "Hey, it's me. I'll be a few minutes late. See you there." A married woman I was seeing at that time had left one such message on my machine, and since answering machines played their messages into the whole room back then, Obra heard it.

"Why do women date you?" he asked, making absolutely no attempt to conceal his sarcasm.

"Because I'm a feminist in relationships but a chauvinist in bed." I don't know where that answer came from, but since I was still in a mood to be a smartass, it fit our context.

In spite of our pratfalls and horseplay, Obra seemed distracted. Usually my immaturity lifted his spirits, but not today. It was Saturday afternoon by then, cocktail time as far as I was concerned, so I glassed us up and fire-tipped a cigar. I drink classic gin martinis, extra dry, and always swirled—they should never be shaken or stirred as those beastly Europeans would have us think. Obra drinks margaritas, light on the tequila. He also doesn't smoke cigars. Nobody's perfect.

As I fixed our drinks, I asked Obra a question. I was concentrating on my hands and only halfway paying attention to what I said next.

"Are you distracted today, pal, or is it my imagination?"

We have no idea how a little moment like that can jackknife into a life-changing event. We see a cubist painting in a museum with our classmates, or we take a boat ride with our bosses, or we find a stack of salacious magazines with our cousins, or we ask a girl if she's a virgin …

Any moment can zigzag into bigness without warning. A quiet juncture in time grabs the steering wheel of our destiny and whips us into a brand-new direction.

By asking Obra that question, that absentminded little question, I embarked on one of the major episodes of my life. I was never the same again after that, for soon after asking that question, and because of the answer I received, I organized my first death of a human being. Obra and I did it together. As the erosion of my incorruptibility quickened, this was a big step downward for me.

Murder is a sin, and a big one, but so is blind-eyed, head-in-the-sand injustice. This event may certainly have been the bridge that took me away from my ethos and into my perdition, but I did it for the right reasons. There are pardonable reasons to kill some people, so much so that it even has a name: justifiable homicide. Soldiers get medals for it, but I wasn't a soldier—I was just a guy exercising an individual act of reason based on my ideology and values. I know in my soul of souls that I did the right thing, but still, by that logic, there wouldn't be a human being left on the planet if we could kill people just because we feel they have violated our principles.

Was I a kindhearted person who finally grew a pair of balls and stepped up to make right something that was horribly wrong, or was I just going crazy and this was my excuse for violence? Mothers everywhere would applaud Obra and me for what we did, but unless the jury were twelve angry moms, we would go to prison for life because of our actions. Simple as that.

My drinking increased during this phase of my life by quite a lot. I was able to keep it in the closet, so I didn't get into any booze-related trouble, but I don't think it helped my rational abilities or my health—or my spirituality. What was leading me into these places of darkness? Was I insane? How does one know? Was I chosen? What does God's voice sound like as it tells us to become murderous paladins? Is it an audible voice, or is it only inside our imagination? Moses had a burning bush. All I had was actuation.

CHAPTER 7

Son of Shelomit, the Daughter of Dibri

Thus my guide goes first downward through the spiral, and I go second. "We'll wait a while," my guide tells me, "that our senses will grow accustomed to this vile scent, and after that, it will not trouble us to take our next steps deeper."
—**Dante Alighieri, from *The Divine Comedy*, "Inferno," canto IX**

The short version of the story Obra told me is that there was a woman we both knew, and she and her daughter were raped together by the same guy. It had happened years prior, but I'd not heard about it. I was still in graduate school at the time, so when I wasn't working back then, I was studying. Current events can whiz past us unobserved during periods like that.

Obra said the guy raped and sodomized the mother and daughter in full view of each other and then beat them and left them for dead. The daughter did indeed die, but the mother survived ... sort of.

Obra's news put me in shock. "'How could I not know this?'" I asked.

"Out of respect, it's still pretty hush-hush," Obra answered. "Nobody wants to seem gossipy about something as horrid as this."

"Have the police caught him?"

"No. Last week I asked a cop I know about the case, which is what has it fresh in my mind." I could tell by the way Obra vaguely said "a cop I know" that he didn't want to reveal the police officer's name.

"What did the cop say?" I asked.

"That's what makes it so heinous. Inside information is that this guy is an occasional informant, so when the crime occurred, there was some uncertainty about motivation to actually capture him. By the time those dipshits made up their minds, there were other cases to think about—high-profile cases. Besides, we both know everything depends on who's in vogue."

The woman's name was Andrea Arno. She was an acquaintance of some of the women who worked in my building at the School District offices, and when she came to see them, she usually poked her head into everyone's office just to say hello. The usual topic of conversation when she came into my office was that I needed some plants to decorate the place. I agreed. She said she had too many plants at her house and that she couldn't bear to kill them, so I could have some if I wanted. She even agreed to help nurture the plants if I agreed to put them in my office.

Some of the plants Andrea gave me thrived, but some of them appeared to be suffering, so I went to her house two or three times, exchanging them until I had plants that seemed to like me.

"I'm impressed that you would give potted plants that much consideration rather than just let them die," she said.

"If we take control of a living thing, even a plant in a pot, then we should put forth a good-faith effort to take care of that thing," I said.

Every now and again, Andrea would come into my office and fuss with the plants. While she was there, she would tell me about her daughter. She even had a nickname for the kid. It was "Waif."

Andrea was the picture of perfect parenting. She also had one and a half arms. I mention the missing half arm because I think losing half an arm made Andrea a more attentive parent—not so much because of the absence of her hand, but because of the way it happened.

She was a child when she lost her arm, riding a lawnmower along with her sister on their mother's lap. At first the mother was entertaining the girls by riding in aimless loops around the yard, but after a while, she thought she'd turn on the blade and cut a little grass while they were at it. They passed through a cloud of gnats, and the girls panicked. Amid all the screaming and flailing, Andrea's sister smacked their mother in the face, disorienting the woman and sending her glasses flying. The mother impulsively lunged for the glasses to keep them from landing on the ground and getting run over by the mower. When she sprang to catch the glasses, she lost control of the girls. The result was tragic.

There was never mention of a man in Andrea's life. I'm sure she had family somewhere, but none of them lived right there in the house with her, and I could only imagine how lonely the place must be now that the girl was dead.

People react to shocking information in different ways. In my case, I had to get revenge for Andrea.

There are several things Louisiana has to offer that are immeasurably greater than those in any other place on earth. Among them are stylish women, excellent food, Catahoula leopard cur dogs, and Cajun justice. The women and the food are well known, but you have to live in Louisiana to understand the dogs and the justice. The code is still Napoleonic.

Cajun justice is the thing that's relevant to this diary because it involves taking the law into one's own hands, which is what I did—first with Obra for Andrea Arno, and then later on my own. In situations of Cajun justice, friends and family straighten out things in direct response to the wrongs done unto them. The process is camouflaged and quiet, but close so you can get to it quickly just in case you need it. *Zip, bang, boom!* Eye-for-eye reciprocity. All's well that ends well.

Obra and I developed a simple Cajun justice plan to seek retribution for Andrea and her daughter. The plan involved the swapping of a couple of favors and the disposal of some trash. It was the perfect three-point endeavor.

First, I contacted a man I knew named Simoniac. He was one of those guys who liked to talk and listen, so he knew a lot about who did what. If it's true that all politics are local, then guys like Simoniac are the reason why. I'd recently heard his daughter had been denied admission into a prominent New Orleans university, and that information was useful to me. I called Simoniac about a trumped-up central office issue, and while we were on the phone, I asked him how his daughter was doing. He gave me the news of his daughter's rejection from the university, and I told him I had a friend who had a friend who worked there. I said I would be glad to inquire about the daughter's rejection to see exactly what happened.

Obra has a buyer named Barrator at the university. Obra's buyers like to keep him happy, so when he called the buyer and inquired about the girl's failed application, wonder of wonders, wouldn't you know it—they determined that a mistake had, in fact, been made. Imagine that!

A new letter from Barrator accepting Simoniac's daughter into the university was in the mail almost before the two of them hung up their telephones. Simoniac now owed us a favor.

When I called Simoniac with the news, he told me he wasn't sure what I had done, but he appreciated it, and he said he had a very good memory for people who did him favors. I told him I would prefer that his memory be short because I wanted some information, and after he gave me the information, I wanted him to forget he ever heard of the subject. I told him I wanted a name. I told him I wanted the name of someone who had done a terrible thing. He understood and agreed.

I should pause here and say that I've reflected on that phone call obsessively over the years. As superficial and matter-of-fact as the event may seem, it's actually of tremendous importance in documenting my moral decay and feelings of emotional turmoil because, by making that phone call, I had for the first time in my life set into motion my own deliberate scheme to activate a plan of illegality. I dabbled in the waters of deception and found the experience to be pleasant. We do not lose the fight between good and evil all at once; it happens gradually over time, sometimes beginning with one simple phone call. Even after all I have done, I've agonized over making that phone call ever since the moment I hung up the receiver.

I asked Simoniac for the name of the man who raped Andrea Arno and killed her daughter. A couple of days later, Simoniac called me back and said we should meet face-to-face about my request. At that meeting, he gave me a name. The name was Geryon. It was an old Cajun name, not really all that common anymore, but every once in a while someone still crawls out of the Atchafalaya Basin just long enough to have a baby at the Ochsner Free Clinic and give it an anachronistic name like "Geryon."

"Are you positive?" I asked Simoniac.

"Yes, positive," he replied.

"There's been a little buzz about him, so I need to be sure you're not basing your research on that hearsay or gossip."

"No, I'm not," Simoniac said. "I triangulated my information. He's the guy who raped Andrea Arno and killed her daughter." That was that. We had our man.

Obra and I needed a place in the woods to deal with Geryon. I took Obra to a place I knew. We went through a pathless wood and set up camp on the abominable sand at the edge of a pier—the Pier delle Vigne. I knew for a fact we would be isolated, for I had studied the area before.

"This place is perfect for what we need, but how in the world did you ever find it?" Obra asked. "This looks like a graveyard where dinosaurs came to die!" My friend had no idea. I left things that way.

After a period of planning and preparation, we were ready for the big event. We casually asked Andrea to join us at the campsite. We told her we had been camping at this beautiful place, and we invited her to stop by and see it. We told her that she was welcome to stay the night with us, or she could just stop by for an evening meal and leave when she wanted.

"Closest I've ever come to camping is to toss twigs into the chiminea on my deck," she joked. Being too polite for a direct refusal, she was sidestepping our invitation without having to reject it.

At first, Andrea of course declined, but Obra and I kept asking until she agreed. We almost pleaded with her, and it was only the promise that she would have a great meal and see some astoundingly beautiful plant life that finally won her over. Even though our invitation to join us at a campsite was a little odd, I think Andrea agreed mostly because she wanted to get out of the house and be among some pleasant people. Sometimes boredom is our strongest motivator. We just need to see new sights and breathe new air. Besides, Andrea had been with me in my office chatting about plants for several years by then, and she'd known Obra's family all her life, so I imagine she felt secure enough to accept our invitation.

I estimate that Andrea was not quite a decade older than I was at the time—probably midforties or so, or maybe a few years older than that. She was one of those people who had a perpetually youthful persona, and that made her age difficult to guess.

Andrea was big in a lot of ways. She was tall and heavy, and she had huge breasts and a tremendous heart. I know hearts aren't really part of someone's appearance, but hers was. She was one of those people who had such a big spirit that it radiated.

Andrea had thick red hair and bright green eyes. She had beautiful skin: lily white mixed with auburn ginger. It was kind of luminous. Her face was covered in freckles. She had an infectious laugh and shared it generously. She often joked that she wanted a lot of freckles to distract people from staring at her chubby body but that it didn't work when she was walking away. She said that if someone told her to haul ass, she'd have to make two trips. We all loved her self-deprecating humor and her contagiously positive energy. If ever there was a gift from heaven to mortal people, Andrea teaching us to laugh at ourselves was it.

Andrea especially glowed when she talked about her daughter. She talked like the girl was the one thing she lived for, the thing she truly loved and cherished, and the thing she displayed as a symbol of all the good that life had to offer. Geryon took that away. He took the one thing she really loved and lived for. He held it right in front of her face, and then he tortured her with it. He used it against her. He tried to kill her with the act. He failed. My, my, me!

Armed with the information Simoniac gave us, Obra and I went to get Geryon. It was a Saturday afternoon when we started.

Geryon was easy to identify. As most egomaniacs will do, he liked to talk loudly, and he didn't mind giving up a fact or two about his secret deeds just to be the center of attention. I've always considered it sadly ironic that the more ignorant the people, the louder the voice they use, and the more they talk about themselves.

We met Geryon and started a conversation. We knew he would slit our throats for the spare change in our pockets, so we were careful. We tossed a couple of compliments at him and encouraged him to talk about himself, so he seemed to enjoy having us around. Our conversation was totally about him, so I imagine he probably thought we were geniuses.

Geryon was playing pool in a bar. The place was probably busy on Saturday evenings, but since we were there midafternoon, only a few regulars milled around the place. All Obra and I had to do was walk up and put a quarter on the pool table to get him to notice us. A quarter is what it cost to play a game of pool at that time, and putting one on the edge of a pool table was the standard message that we were next to play. Geryon informed us that we were mistaken. We withdrew our money and apologized. Contact had been made, and conversation soon followed.

Geryon walked in a way so odd that it symbolized volumes about his personality. It was part saunter and part strut, as if he had something important to say and was about to stop and say it every time he took a step. It literally looked as though he was going to stop on each step but then decided to creep along just a little bit more, so he seemed to be skulking and lounging at the same time, studying people and sizing up each situation as he strolled into it. His slow-motion advance had a condescending aura, and each halting step communicated self-satisfaction. His eyes had a pig-trough smugness about them—a half-shut smirk with a know-it-all sneer, as if he had just caught all us silly little people at our misdeeds, so now we were subject to his whimsical retribution.

The two things Geryon liked to talk about were himself and sex, so those became our topics of conversation. We hinted that a real man can have sex whenever he wants it, and he can have it with anyone he wants—even groups of people. He asked if we were interested, and we said it depended on our moods and who else was involved. He stopped and looked at us with a sickening kind of hopefulness.

I told him I had a fantasy about group sex with people who are related—sisters, mothers, and daughters ... things like that. It was a change in rhythm from our conversational pattern for me to initiate a topic, not to mention telling a bald-faced lie, so I worried Geryon would notice and break off our connection, but he didn't. I know that psychos tend to be overly sensitive to subtleties, but I had to bring up the subject somehow. I guess Geryon's ego overpowered his paranoia, so he told us about it—a mother and a daughter. He said he'd made them watch. He said he had a lot of manhood to offer, and that when he was finished, they were just little puddles of used-up women. He snickered with a wheezy chuckle as he said the words, and it took all my willpower to not attack him with my pool cue right then in the bar. He said he was more than most people could take, and his partners were usually never the same again. He said it was the price they paid for having genuine sex.

Talking to Geryon about his sexuality was hard to endure but easy to sustain. All we had to do was keep the topic about him, but I almost blew it once when a Yat came in asking for a backhouse terlet. Without hesitation, I gave the guy directions. I should have kept my mouth shut, because communication like that requires foreknowledge and commonality, and Geryon noticed. For crazy people like him, there's no such thing as a mood of relaxed curiosity, because insanity isn't capable of remaining calm while thinking. In twisted brains, awareness embroils instantaneously into suspicion and aggression. Feeling threatened by all situations not of their own design, they experience a sell-to-the-table purging of emotions that takes them down to combat instincts. I didn't want his mind to go there, but it did.

Geryon stopped moving and turned to look straight at me while I was taking aim on the pool table, so I quickly popped the cue ball over the foot-string diamond where he was leaning against the rail. I wanted the cue ball to hit him to distract him further, but he caught it in midflight. That turned out to be even better, because it gave him a cool air of bragging rights. Preoccupied with exercising those rights, he totally forgot about the Yat and repositioned his brain on himself.

"Good catch! You have catlike reflexes," I said.

"You're a terrible shot."

"You're very good at this game."

"I'm going to take your money," he added with a coughing laugh and a vainglorious smirk in his eyes. "I won't even have to try."

By the way, Yats are known for their smart-alecky, I'm-better-than-you bravado, so I was worried that on his way out the door, the guy I talked to might stop by the table with an imperious lesson about how to shoot pool. He must have been in a hurry to leave, because after he used the bathroom, he walked inconspicuously out the door.

Obra and I soon put the final phase of our plan into effect. We invited Geryon outside for some Molly, and the poor bastard didn't hesitate. We walked him to our pickup truck, substituted a Rohypnol pill for ecstasy, and hauled his sorry ass to the campsite. It was as simple as that. By the time we got there, he was out cold.

We stripped Geryon naked, wrapped him in sheets like a mummy, and frapped him with duct tape to the top of several eight-foot two-by-four boards to form a kind of stretcher.

"That was an amazing shot you made at the pool table," Obra said while we were working.

"It went better than I planned."

We taped Geryon's mouth shut so he couldn't yell for help when he woke up. The only things we left uncovered were his eyes for seeing and his nose for breathing. We even taped his head to the boards so he couldn't turn his face from side to side. He could only lie there, facing straight up and breathing through his nose. By the light of our lanterns, he looked very much like an Egyptian mummy, wrapped in sheets and taped to a board stretcher.

In spite of Geryon's bulk, Obra and I could use the leverage of the eight-foot boards to move him around with relative ease. Obra can't lift much, so I did most of the work. We put the head-end of Geryon's stretcher up onto two layers of concrete blocks, and then we lifted the feet-end up and put more concrete blocks under that end so Geryon was stretched knee-high between them, as if on a bench.

I started putting firewood under Geryon while Obra went to get Andrea. It was getting to be near suppertime by then, and Andrea would be hungry.

We planned for Andrea to meet us at a local gas-and-snack that was just a few miles from the campsite. She said she didn't mind driving all the way to the campsite so we wouldn't have to come out of the woods and get her, but we told her she would never find the place by herself. That was the reason we gave her, and it's true, but it's not complete.

The bigger reason we wanted to meet Andrea away from the campsite was to be sure that she didn't bring anyone else with her—or lead them there. It was entirely likely that she could experience a stroke of last-minute timidity and decide she needed to bring a companion along with her for assurance.

We didn't need to take that precaution, for Andrea was waiting at the gas station completely alone when Obra arrived. He said she parked off to the side of the lot and climbed into the pickup truck without hesitation.

Obra soon returned with Andrea. I saw their headlights through the trees, and I walked to the parking area to greet them. "Nice skiff," Andrea said to me as we walked into the campsite. She was looking at my little wooden pirogue propped against a tree. I had been so preoccupied with other things that I had forgotten about it. Obra went to check on Geryon.

"Thanks," I replied.

"You don't see many wooden boats anymore," Andrea said. Her voice was smooth.

"No," I responded. "This is the aluminum era. Wooden boats are high maintenance, and the only thing that makes them worth having is that they're charming and beautiful."

"The added upkeep doesn't bother you?" Andrea asked. She was making polite conversation, but I think she was also genuinely interested in the skiff. And my personality.

"No ma'am," I answered. "The best things in life are always a pain in the ass." She looked at me and laughed. I don't think a lot of people say words like "ass" to Andrea.

"I like the poesy of your reasoning," she said with a chuckle.

While Obra was gone, Andrea and I made small talk. I like to spend time in the woods, so I have a lot of camping gear, and Andrea was interested in it. I also have quite a bit of outdoor cooking equipment, and Andrea was interested in that as well. She asked if I spent many Saturday nights camping, and I told her yes, when I could, adding that it was a good way to stay out of trouble but that until recently my studies at the university took most of my weekends. I told her about the many pleasant days I spent in the woods with my cousins as a child and that those feelings of peace carried over into my adulthood.

After that, I took Andrea to where our makeshift bathroom was located up the path. I wasn't sure she would stay with us long enough to use any of these things, but I wanted her to know about her options. Besides, the tour seemed like a good way to make her feel at home. Sometimes the gesture of a thing is more important than its actual practicality.

"Why aren't you married, Mark?" Andrea asked abruptly. When she asked, I looked at her. Her eyes were fixed on the ground off to my side, but she didn't seem to be thinking about the place where her eyes were focused. The question was sudden, and it startled me a little. I then knew what she meant a few minutes earlier about camping on Saturday nights. Sometimes I can be a little slow to catch a conversation. In spite of being caught off-guard by it all, I gave her a clear-headed answer.

"Because, ma'am," I told her, "this is the age of aluminum for relationships just as much as it is for boats, and I am a boat made of wood."

"Some women like that in a man," she said.

"Not for long," I replied. I wasn't joking, so there was a little more retort in my comeback than I intended, and an awkward pause ensued.

"Where did Obra wander off to?" Andrea asked, a little clumsily. She pulled her eyes off the ground and looked around the bayou.

CHAPTER 8

Dia de los Muertos

When a fit request is made, it ought to be followed by work in silence.
—Dante Alighieri, from *The Divine Comedy*, "Inferno," canto XXIV

ndrea and I walked in silence to meet Obra at the campsite, and the three of us started to visit about a variety of things. In spite of what Obra and I knew lay ahead, our conversation was light and happy, just the way we intended. We soon sat to eat.

For our entrée, I grilled bacon-wrapped popcorn shrimp crusted thinly with a glaze of pineapple, brown sugar, and honey. I also grilled asparagus that had been marinating in zesty Italian dressing. We sipped blackberry wine.

Later, after we finished most of the meal and the mood seemed to be right, we mentioned Andrea's daughter, Waif. We did it casually while we sipped petite glasses of ice-cold Creole lemon sherry and ate dark-roasted cashews dipped in chocolate.

I had a six-inch cast-iron skillet about half full of melted chocolate beside the fire, and another pot roasting cashews nearby. Andrea spooned small amounts of chocolate onto a paper plate and swirled each of her cashews through it with care. She was deft for having only one hand. I kept tossing little bits of chocolate into the pan, so there was always just a slight amount remaining. Funny thing about chocolate: if there's a lot of it, then we can leave it alone, but if there's just a little bit more, we have to eat it. That's the law.

These two cast-iron pans are among my favorites, so we talked about them. They're family heirlooms. That conversation seemed to relax Andrea, so I volunteered plenty of details. She expressed interest in cast-iron cookery, but I think she also wanted to learn about my family.

"A man on his own seems to attract a woman's attention," she said by way of excusing her interrogation, "Even if we're not in the market for one."

As with most of Louisiana, the vegetation is very thick where we were camping, so even though Geryon wasn't far from us, Andrea couldn't see him from where we were situated. Also, in spite of our small fire and frequent laughter, it would be difficult for others to detect us.

Andrea looked into the fire as she talked about Waif. Obra and I wanted to get some sense of how she would feel about our plans for Geryon, but as it turns out, it seemed good for her to talk, so we let the conversation linger.

"After what happened," she said, "most people avoid talking about Waif, but I can see the curiosity in their eyes. It's as though they're silently begging me for the inside scoop. I want to slap them. They want to dish, and it's offensive to me because I don't want to gossip about my daughter's death. But she did live, and I do want to remember her, so I like to talk about her life."

Our plans for Geryon were going to happen whether Andrea was involved or not, but we did need to know how she felt before we involved her. When she told us she would like to kill the man who did those things, Obra and I decided to include her in our deeds.

"Do you really mean that, Andrea?"

"Yes," she said after a thoughtful pause. "I really would like to kill him—literally. And I know exactly how I would do it."

As part of our plans, Obra and I had agreed way ahead of time that the first meeting of Andrea and Geryon would be delicate, so we decided that if it actually happened, I would concentrate on Geryon, and Obra would watch Andrea. That way, neither of them would be unobserved during those first few moments. Because I was watching

Geryon, I'm not sure what Andrea's initial reaction was when she first saw him. His reaction, however, will be in my mind forever.

Geryon was awake as we walked toward him. I think he had just recently awakened, because he seemed to still be trying to comprehend the details of his predicament. It was totally dark by then, and he used the approaching light of our lanterns to study his surroundings. He wasn't exactly struggling, so I don't think he yet knew the full extent of his limitations. His eyes strained to look around the corners of his skull to study our approach. He was trying to say something, but under all that duct tape, his voice just sounded like a dog barking miles away.

As the three of us stood there looking at him, his eyes darted around the campsite to try to take in details. I don't think he liked the setup very much, but weirdly, neither was he expressing panic. Projecting my psychological normalcy upon him, I assumed he would be in a freak at that moment, but he wasn't. He was still muttering something, but his voice was quieter. Obra and I looked around to be sure there weren't any changes or surprises nearby, and then we both looked at Andrea. She just stood there for a minute or two, which seemed like a half hour, and then she slowly walked toward Geryon.

Although Obra and I had never really discussed it, I think we were both expecting her to ask us a whole bunch of questions and then break into a full run and attack Geryon, but she didn't do either of those things. She just stood beside us silently for a little while and then slowly walked forward like a kid on Christmas morning who can't believe the bike is actually under the tree. The simile is accurate, and it didn't occur to me until the moment I wrote these words that we really had made a gift of this guy. We wrapped him up and delivered him to her just like a present. I can hear Kevin Bruce smiling even as I recall these details.

The original plan at that point was to let Andrea beat on Geryon until she was satisfied or exhausted, and then we were going to help her set him on fire. It didn't exactly go that way.

What happened is Andrea stood beside him, humming softly. It sounded hauntingly like *Pop Goes the Weasel*. Her arms were wrapped under her large breasts, cradling them.

Obra nudged my elbow to wake me from my stupor, and we moved quietly to a nearby tree and sat on the ground, leaning against it. The three of us were still comfortably hidden from the outside world by thick vegetation—four of us, if you count Geryon.

Suddenly Andrea amazed us. We glanced quickly at each other for validation and then neck-snap looked back at her. Andrea was taking off her clothes!

The first thing she took off was her shoes. She wasn't wearing socks, and she easily slipped off each shoe by pressing the toe of one foot against the heel of the other. It took her about one second for each shoe. She bent from the waist, picked up the shoes, and carefully put them off to the side. I remember them clearly. They were white canvas sneakers.

Andrea then unsnapped her jeans, unzipped them, and pulled them off her legs. She carefully folded her jeans and laid them on top of her shoes. Her movements were commonplace to the extent of being surreal, but what made it even more so was the way Andrea was acting: she was thoroughly calm and slow. Her movements were balanced and smooth, and she was still softly humming. She looked as if she had been in this very circumstance every day of her life.

Obra and I have since then discussed the possibility that Andrea may have actually rehearsed this situation in her mind. She told us a little earlier that she knew how she would kill Geryon if she had the chance, but I think we underestimated the extent to which she thought about the details. Now that he was there, her emotional autopilot kicked in. I was feeling humble for assuming that Andrea would need us to guide her through this encounter. Compared to her experience, my life was tiny. Who was I to think I could help her?

While I was having these thoughts, Andrea slipped off her white cotton panties. She was alone in the universe with her thoughts and her goals, and having us sitting there twenty feet away, propped against a tree, meant nothing at all to her. I think she had forgotten about everything except her plans for Geryon's destiny. She laid the panties on top of her folded jeans.

By this time, Andrea was naked from the waist down. Only her cotton blouse and bra remained. She unbuttoned the blouse and let it fall open; then she reached behind her back with her one hand to unhook her bra. She took off the bra without removing her blouse by slipping the straps through her sleeves and over her elbows. She leaned slightly forward and pulled the bra off her breasts, folded it, and carefully laid it with her other clothes. Her red hair and luminescent ginger skin glowed in the lantern-lit darkness.

Andrea slowly walked in a circle around the mummified Geryon. She strolled lingeringly, lap after lap, each circumference a little smaller and tighter than the one before. The firewood I had previously tucked under Geryon started to get in her way, so she removed it. As she approached each piece, she picked it up and tossed it gently off to the side. She bent straight-legged from the waist, giving Geryon a full view of her large breasts swinging brazenly out the front of her unbuttoned blouse.

After a few minutes, Andrea had removed almost all the firewood from under Geryon's makeshift stretcher. Was she saving him from the fire? This thought made me nervous. I didn't know what Geryon was thinking, and I surely didn't know about Andrea, but I did know what I was thinking. I was thinking that if Andrea slipped off the high-dive of sanity, I needed to remain completely aware of our surroundings to do what Obra and I had planned. Aside from the fact that we hated him, Geryon wasn't the kind of guy we wanted as a living, talking enemy, so we knew he could never leave that campsite alive. Andrea might have wigged out, but I was still of sound mind.

Soon Andrea started talking to Geryon. Strangely, this comforted me. I guess I figured that if she was coherent enough to verbalize her thoughts, then we knew we could talk to her if need be. The only problem was that she wasn't really talking; she was just repeating the same three words over and over again: "I want it!" As she said the words, her eyes were fixated upon Geryon's fully engorged groin, which was straining noticeably against the tightness of the sheets.

Andrea walked to Geryon's side and stood by his thighs. She squatted to sit on her heels and reached for his erection. I expected her to be violent with it, but she wasn't. She just reached for it slowly, and she very lightly scratched it through the sheets with her fingernails. To this day, I can hear her fingernails on those sheets. Truth be told, the sound haunts me a little.

I had ceased to be amazed. I think a spaceship could have landed right there on the Pier delle Vigne near us and I would hardly have blinked. People can take only so much shock before they reach their capacity for additional reaction.

After a moment or two of stroking his erection, Andrea stood and walked to Geryon's head. She stood over it, straddling it, with the inside of her knees beside each of his ears. He was looking calmly but wondrously up into her body, searching into the depths of her pelvis.

Obra and I looked at each other and talked softly. The only thing that kept us from intervening was the knowledge that Geryon was securely bound and that Andrea was apparently having a therapeutic catharsis.

"If Andrea starts to undo Geryon's wrap, then we should intercede," I softly said.

"Okay, but until then, we should just sit quietly and watch."

"I agree."

However roundabout Andrea went, she seemed to be purging something vile, and we didn't want to interrupt the exorcism. She pressed Geryon's face with her knees as she patiently stood there rocking from side to side. Whatever her motivation, she was clearly letting him achieve his visual fill.

As I looked at Geryon and Andrea together, for the first time I wondered about his past. I knew her story, so I sympathized with it, but what about Geryon? Would any of his story inspire compassion if only we knew of it? I could see Andrea's demon—Obra and I had captured it and bound it in a sheet and delivered it to her in the woods—but I wondered what Geryon's demon looked like. What twisted events had shattered his normalcy? Did anyone wrap Geryon's chimera and deliver it to him as a gift of reckoning? Did his monster go unpunished, or did it pay as costly a penalty as he himself was about to render?

Knowing I can tell Pat about my past without fear of prosecution, I've communicated to her all the details of this event, yet something bothers me still about her reaction. Of all the bizarre details I described, the only questions she asked were about what I've communicated here in that last paragraph—the part where I wondered about Geryon's demons. That seems odd to me, but hey, I'm not the one who's a trained therapist.

Continuing to give Geryon's eyeballs a first-class ride, Andrea squatted by his head and stroked his face, whispering to him. Then she started to crawl down his body toward his erection. She moved slowly, crawling with a sort of lurching irregularity due to the uneven length of her arms. In spite of that, she was smooth as she rolled forward and skulked across Geryon's torso to his groin. The boards were still set on the concrete blocks as she spider-crawled her way over the top of him. Her huge breasts dragged against his body for nearly every inch of the journey. She skimmed herself with special care across his eyes and nose as she moved—first her hair, then her breasts, and then, finally, her pelvis. She seemed to deliberately prolong the brushing of her red pubic hair against his eyes and nose.

Andrea and Geryon were both in a trance. They appeared to be thinking they were on the verge of getting something they wanted very badly.

After a moment, Andrea slowly sat fully upright on Geryon's chest, her tailbone against his chin, and her arms hanging relaxed at her sides. She arched her back inward, a little more than perfectly straight, and she leaned her head back. Artfully and sensually, she pushed her hair back across her shoulders from the front of her neck, and there she sat, face-up, calmly looking at the sky and ethereally rocking her head from side to side. Her thick red hair brushed softly against the back of her neck and shoulders.

Andrea then gently turned her arms out away from her sides and slowly raised them, fully extended, up into the air. Her arms were straight and her elbows locked. The pathos of her prayerful gesture seemed augmented by her missing hand. The fingers on her full arm were lazily curled inward, totally relaxed.

Andrea stopped lifting when her forearms were slightly higher than her head, and she looked as though she was communicating with something in the sky. She was either praising it or asking it a question. I couldn't tell, but the moment was very expressive. It seemed to last a thousand years.

In reality, Andrea stayed like that for not more than a dozen seconds, and then she calmly brought her forearms together over her head. Her arms remained straight and fully extended, and her elbows were still locked. She slowly wrapped the fingers of her one hand around the stumped wrist of her other arm, and then she did the only fast and violent thing yet: she smashed her joined arms into Geryon's groin three times, swinging powerfully downward with her entire upper body. She hit him so hard that the boards actually bounced beneath the two of them. Obra and I jumped from the recoil all three times.

After a few minutes, Geryon quit coughing. Andrea was still sitting on his chest, which probably didn't help. When he recuperated, she lifted her fanny and repositioned her feet so that she was standing straight-legged astraddle of his neck, her pelvis again positioned above his face.

Andrea then bent forward from the waist, still straight legged, to rub Geryon's recovering penis. She rested her weight on her one hand and used the arm with no hand to rub his shaft. When the man's erection had once again achieved its former glory, Andrea bent her neck downward and lowered her face between her pendulous breasts to look back between her thighs at his eyes. He seemed captivated by the view, and she taunted him a little by shaking her pelvis and fanny, twerk style.

All that while, Andrea never stopped concentrating on Geryon's face. She never unlocked her eyes from his.

"Hey!" Andrea suddenly barked, "I want it!" At those words, she had his full attention. Ours too.

I think Geryon was surprised to find that inside Andrea's body was a real person able to say words to him. I'm not sure he knew that about women in general, and until she spoke to him in that commanding tone, he may not have known it about Andrea. He was about to learn.

Andrea was looking down under her body at his face when she said that to him, and then she slowly rolled her face forward to look at his engorged penis again. The thing bulged the sheets. Geryon seemed to be actually having a good time. I guess that, in a head-screwed way, this was his idea of great sex. He had an abusive, dominant, naked woman, and he had an audience. He might have even thought this was prelude to something we would all do later. Recalling what Obra and I had discussed with him at the pool table, I realized we might have planted that expectation.

Andrea reached forward with her hand to squeeze-hold his shaft while she supported her torso on her stump of an arm. She then rolled the center of her back upward toward the sky so that she could aim her pelvis directly at his nose and eyes between her knees, then she slowly lowered herself down fully onto his face.

Andrea suctioned herself onto Geryon's nostrils with the combined weight of every mother who ever had a daughter suffer at the hands of a man. She never took her hand off his erection until he was thoroughly dead.

CHAPTER 9

Brueghel's Icarus

Thou strivest to see too far amid these glooming shadows. Too long a space of darkness has thine eye to traverse. If thou drawest nearer to your purpose, thou wilt see well how much the sense is deceived at a distance. A little more, therefore, I urge thee on.
—Dante Alighieri, from *The Divine Comedy*, "Inferno," canto XXXI

After a minute of being absolutely sure she had completely smothered Geryon, Andrea removed herself from his face, stood up, walked to her clothes, and calmly dressed. She kept her back turned to Obra and me the entire time. Considering what she had just finished doing right there in front of us, her modesty seemed unnecessary and out of place. We did not budge from our seated positions.

After Andrea dressed, she walked near to us and sat against a tree of her own. She looked relaxed—more relaxed than I've ever seen her.

"What now?" she eventually asked. Her voice was calm, delicate, and tired. It sounded resigned, but in a good way.

"We take you home and then we clean up the mess," Obra said. Andrea turned her face to focus on us.

"That's it?" she asked, softly puzzled. "You're not going to tell the police?"

I waited a second before I responded to her question, and I pronounced my reply quietly and simply, intentionally keeping it soft and slow. "No" is all I said.

Andrea looked at us at first with confusion, and then a sweet, graceful understanding dawned in her eyes. "Thank you both," she said after a pause. Her words were velvety and clear.

I don't know if I've ever felt as amateurish in the presence of natural-born greatness as I did right then. If ever I find myself in a foxhole under fire, I want my partner to be Andrea Arno.

After we recuperated, we offered to take Andrea back to her car. She said that sounded nice. She said she needed to take the longest shower of her life and then sleep for a couple of days.

Obra then said, "Andrea, it probably doesn't need to be spoken outright, but we need to make clear that nobody should ever talk about any of this again—especially if someone comes along and asks you straightforward about this guy. He's a piece of shit, and nobody is going to care that he's gone, but his disappearance may inspire some curiosity in the future."

"Done!" she said definitively. The actual word came out of her mouth only, but its intensity clearly came from deeper within her being. It was a terminal tone, but the way she flicked her forearms downward when she spoke is what comforted me most of all. We didn't have to worry. This was one act of kindness that would go unpunished.

"Do you need any help cleaning?" she asked.

"No. We prefer to take care of it ourselves."

Andrea seemed relieved. She glanced at the stacks of firewood around the campsite and at all the little holes, and she seemed to comprehend our disposal plan.

Obra and I thought about both of us taking Andrea to her car, but since the deed was done and Geryon was lying dead at our campsite, we decided one of us should stay there to keep an eye on things. In all our careful planning, we had neglected the details of the aftermath, which is a sign of being first-time assassins. It's a mistake I would not repeat in years to come. There is always an "after" that follows the achievement of reaching a summit, and experienced people know to prepare their downhill muscles for the task of subsiding after the climb. Underestimating downhill travel by misinterpreting it as coasting is a rookie's mistake, and that's why novice killers get caught in that phase.

We decided I would be the one to drive Andrea back to her car while Obra stayed alone at the campsite. I dropped Andrea at her car and drove back, looking for anything out of the ordinary along the way. I didn't see anything odd. All was right with the world.

After I got back to Obra, we made quick work of things. We dragged my little wooden skiff through the pathless wood and across the abominable sand to the pier—the Pier delle Vigne. We put Geryon into the boat and filled it with concrete blocks, and then we chained the concrete blocks and Geryon to the boat. I cut a nearby sapling oak with an axe, and I then put the axe and the sapling into the boat with Geryon and climbed into it myself. The sapling was probably ten feet long, maybe more, and I used it to push us through the shallow water and out into the swamp. Obra stayed at the camp, rekindled the fire, and burned anything that Geryon might have touched.

When the water deepened enough that the sapling wouldn't touch bottom any more, I cast it off to the side, picked up the axe, and chopped the hull of my little wooden pirogue full of holes. I stood upright in it with my life vest on, and when the boat sank out from under me, I released the axe to let it disappear with the rest of my jetsam. I floated away into the warm, warm waters of the bayou.

Following the release of the axe, I didn't move a muscle for quite some time. In that motionless state, I felt as placid as I've ever been. I don't know how long I floated that way in my life vest, but the feeling was wonderful, and I didn't want it to end. In the spirit of baptismal acts, I had drowned my demons, and I felt renewed.

After my period of rest, I propelled myself to the sound of Obra working at the campsite by fluttering with my feet and sweep-steering with my hands and arms. Since I was in no rush and had been gone quite a little while already during the performance of my task, I expected Obra to comment on the delay. He didn't.

Nature is genuinely wild in the bayou. Within the space of just a little while, things dematerialize, which is exactly what I liked about Pier delle Vigne when I found it the first time. Time dissolves what the critters don't eat—which is not much, because there are creatures of every imaginable size and appetite out there. Some of them are big enough to swallow you outright, and some are so small we can't even see them while they masticate us by the millions.

No offence to Andrea, but we never did intend to bury Geryon in the holes. We just wanted her to see the holes so she would think that was the plan. If she got religion in the future and took the authorities back to that exact location, all we wanted them to find were holes filled with ashes and dirt and the bones of our meals. An ounce of prevention is worth a lifetime of being in prison.

Speaking of cautions, Obra and I agreed we would not ever return to Pier delle Vigne. I have never violated that pact, and I stake my reputation that neither did Obra.

Andrea's artistry was deliberate, and she did to Geryon exactly what he had done to her and to Waif. Nothing more. That's what makes it appropriate. Violent sex was to him what Andrea's daughter was to her. It was the one thing Geryon lived for, the one thing he truly loved and cherished—the thing he displayed as a symbol of all the good that life had to offer. Andrea took that all away from him. She took the one thing he really loved and lived for. She held it right in front of his face, and then she tortured him with the act. She used it against him. She tried to kill him with it. She succeeded. My, my, me!

If you don't think what Andrea Arno did was right, then you haven't been beaten, raped, and sodomized right in front of your daughter while she was being beaten, raped, sodomized, and murdered right in front of you. Andrea's boundaries of acceptable behavior were more overarching than what the rest of us have a right to claim, and Obra and I had been commissioned as moral agents within that expanded jurisdiction.

I never intended to kill anyone again, and honest to God, that's the truth, but a seed of justice and purpose had been planted in my mind. I liked it.

Not long after Geryon's murder, I quit my job at the School District. As I write these words, that was a decade and a half ago. Pat says it's important for me to be specific, but it's been so long that I'm having to sit and think about exactly how much time had passed between orchestrating Geryon's death and the end of my traditional career. If not for Pat's encouragement, I wouldn't think about any of those details. I was following the advice Obra gave me on Charon's boat: I was waking up every day and asking what I could do of value right then without trying to make an overarching picture by connecting the dots over time.

My departure from the Florentine Parish School System was of no consequence to anyone but me. I was Brueghel's painting of the fall of Icarus—a tiny pair of legs poking up above the water in an obscure corner of life's landscape while a giant peasant plowed his field on center stage. That vision puts a lot of things into perspective about what's lastingly important in the general scheme of life. The wisdom of *Musee des Beaux Arts* applies to me as much as to Icarus.

By the way, "quit" is the appropriate word for how I departed the school system and my career. I did not retire or resign; I just gave them an Irish goodbye and never went back. Having time to give a little thought to my orbit after that, I soon found other income. It wasn't a career, but it was definitely more purposeful and satisfying day by day. I did not ever consider suicide again. Not once.

There's only one part that puzzles me about Geryon and Andrea and Waif: how did they first meet? If ever there was an oil-and-water situation that should repel people from each other, their personalities were it. That question bothers me still.

Geryon was a monster, proudly displaying his tomial tooth as a badge for all to see, but that's not the way it always goes; evil changes shape and takes many forms. Those new shapes and forms aren't always easy to discern as being dangerous. Nobody ever caught a fish by putting something rebarbative on the hook. Sometimes evil looks and smells like a monster, as Geryon did, but sometimes evil is sugar and spice and everything nice. Deceit is a powerful thing.

CHAPTER 10

Cast-Off Blood and Tea Leaves

Both force and fraud perpetuate harm to others, but since mankind
alone is capable of fraud, it is to God more displeasing. The fraudulent
lie lowest, then, and deepest down in Hell. Hypocrites, flatterers,
dealers in sorcery; panders and cheats and all such filthy stuff.
—**Dante Alighieri, from *The Divine Comedy*, "Inferno," canto XIII**

E arly in my career as a killer, an experienced assassin once told
me that the first time we kill someone, it's because we were
called by a need to do it. After that, homicide either makes
us sick and we never do it again, or we like it so much that we look
for more opportunities. The fact that several times already I have
referred to Geryon's death as "my first murder" pretty much shows
which way I went. Apparently I saw my future in those splattered
drops of blood the way a Gypsy might look into the bottom of a
teacup.

Even back in those days when I thought I knew myself, I wondered
where I would stop. If I could kill that first person, who's to say what
new acts of depravity are within me? I still worry, but now with an
added twist. I worry not only that I am losing my mind but also
that I'm a danger to others. Considering my skillset, this is a tenable
apprehension, for I am frightened at what I've become and haunted
by worries about what I might do in the future. Pity I can't tell Pat
about any of these worries. She'd be legally required to notify the
authorities.

The justice and achievement I felt after what Obra and I did for Andrea Arno gave me a sense of satisfaction beyond anything I had ever experienced before in my life. I liked that feeling a lot—so much so that all I could do was question how I was spending my days, particularly at work, which is probably what really motivated me to quit the School District. Reviewing our career motives is a good thing to do, and metacognitive reviews are good questions to ask ourselves, but still, it was an outrageous act for us to kill Geryon, and I was fundamentally wired to be simpleminded, so it troubled me. Somehow I knew all these events were important; I just couldn't put my finger on how or why.

Looking back, I now see that I was changing biologically as much as ideologically, which probably complicated my understanding of things in general. Without my permission, my hormones were evaporating, so I needed a new sextant. Lacking the convenience of a Greek chorus chanting in my ear or a pair of glasses with a chyron on the inside, I had to figure things out on my own.

The career change was good for me, because I wouldn't have thrived working for the School District. I tried my hand at private entrepreneurism. I flourished!

After my job with the school system, I was independently employed. I was Joe Barbecue. That was the name of my business. I went from public school teacher to private business owner.

Being a huckle bearer at the funeral of your own career is an interesting thing. I recommend it because it lets you see the difference between people who were friends with you and people who were friends with your job title.

As I look back at the demise of my career with the school system, I have to confess that toward the end, I deserved what I got. Truth will indeed set you free, but sometimes that freedom comes in the form of unemployment. During my period of transition between public service and private entrepreneurship, I met new people. Not all those relationships were healthy.

One of those relationships was with a man named Fredrick King, but just to bust his chops, I frequently inverted his first and last names into King Frederick—King for short. We exercised together at a local country club.

"Mark, you're the worst racquetball player I've ever known," King said to me one day at the gym. Fred and I would get together regularly back in those days, once or twice a week, for a "friendly" game. He always won.

"What's the score, King?" I asked the question often because it delayed the action while I caught my breath.

"It doesn't matter," he would say. "I'm kicking your ass, and that's all you need to know. You should concentrate. That's why you lose; you don't concentrate on what's important." Frederick King is proof positive that winning inspires superiority, and superiority breeds advice.

Merely winning is never enough for people like Fred. They need to see their opponents suffer, and in that spirit, Fred liked to run his mouth while he defeated me at racquetball. He spoke easily, and he barely showed any effort; yet I, on the other hand, puffed and chugged my titanic way through the game. I was in good shape in those days, but I'm big-boned with disproportionately large shoulders and arms, which is not an asset during games like racquetball.

I asked King many questions. In negotiation, this is a technique known as feinting, which is when you pretend to pursue one topic but you actually want to further your interests in another direction. I was a master at it. I used it on Fred all the time. "You're doing something big at work, aren't you?" I would prod.

Fred could keep a secret about other people, but he liked to brag about himself, and eventually he'd always start talking. He couldn't stop, and through his bragging, he would tell me where he was planning to be and for how long. After I had exercised a little and learned Frederick's whereabouts and plans, I would lose the game as quickly as I could, congratulate him on his superior playing abilities, and then leave his presence. At that point, I would call his wife and make arrangements to bed her. It's relevant to mention that Frederick lorded his presumptuous superiority over her just as he did over me. If you feel omniscient, either you have your hidebound trenches overly memorized or you don't know all the facts. Fred might have been good at gamesmanship, but I was good at alchemy.

Fred's wife is a tiny little Hispanic woman with fondant-smooth, creamy brown skin. She had large, beautiful eyes, oversize lips, and the voice of a child. It was wonderful just to hear her speak. She was born in Mexico and spoke with a crisp, beautiful accent. Her gifts for narrative description are captivating, and listening to her tell of her adventures made me feel as if I had actually been there with her.

My sobriquet for her was "Boulette" because she was small and yummy, and she satisfied my hunger. Sometimes I called her "B" for short. Her real name is Francesca. She didn't take Frederick's last name, so don't bother researching about her that way. When I was feeling playful, I called her "Francesca Boulette." B is older than me by a little over four years, so she called me "Junior."

"Mark," she abruptly asked me one day as I stuffed cotton balls between her toes, preparing to paint her toenails. I could tell she was serious because she called me by my real name. "Why do you spend time with me? Is it just for sex?" She was acting a little blue. I suspect Fred had been at her again and she needed some repair.

"No, it's not just for sex," I answered.

"Then why? You know I'm married and there's no chance of a lasting relationship."

"Because you're like a beloved song that unexpectedly comes on the radio, and because your husband is the type of guy who starts talking when he notices I want to listen to the music."

I guess she enjoyed hearing those things, because it took thirty minutes for me to regain enough strength to stand after the world-class hummer she gave me—which is saying something, since I had the legs of a lumberjack back in those days. She approached me embouchure and dragged me across her alveolar ridge until I landed in a coma. Come to think of it, I may not have ever fully recovered even yet, to this very day. I may have suffered permanent damage, but it was worth it.

When I pause to remember B, I can still feel the tightness of her little body in my hands as she crawled over me during our time together. Except for her enormous and happy nipples, she has absolutely no breasts at all. Another thing I liked about her body is that she has a lot of front-thigh, which is probably my favorite part. Wrapped in a Lucy dress, the fronts of her thighs and her magnificent derriere are among the most beautiful things I've ever seen. She loved to scamper around my condo wearing nothing but panties, which I encouraged. In fact, I spent quite a lot of money buying them for her. She would usually shuck down naked immediately after she walked through my door to put on her new panties. Her favorite thing to do then was climb up the front of me, which I also encouraged. I was benching around three hundred at that time, so it was no strain at all to hold her for a half hour or more while we french kissed and I felt her up. Unlike racquetball, this is the type of circumstance when it is good to be big-boned with disproportionately large shoulders and arms.

Boulette would often wrap her legs around my waist, and we would make out for long, delightful periods of time. Her mouth was as delicious as her lips were large. When she was ready for me to get serious, she would press her nipples into my mouth. That was my signal. As I licked her areolae, I would embrace her petit fours ass, and then I would slip my hands under her new panties and fingertip her into a climax. I could always tell when I was doing things right because she would press her pelvis into my abdomen and boa-constrict those short, beautiful thighs around my ribs. As she was about to peak, her breathing would reach a deep, rhythmic equipoise with the pulsating tightness of her thighs.

We were partners, Boulette and me, collaborating to give her body orgasms, one after another. We had the procedure honed to a science, and we did it a lot. The only variation was what I did to her afterward as she recuperated in a dreamlike stupor.

When she'd had enough, her legs would go limp. It was another of her signals. She would bring her feet together and slide down the front of my body far enough that she could rest her head on my shoulder. With her in that position, feet bouncing against my shins and face relaxed into my neck, I would carry her to the bed and lay her there, gently, like the treasure she is. Oh my, the things I did to her then! Unspeakable, abominable things! It was wonderful. I doubt she remembers any of it.

Each of our visits was almost identical. It was odd but fun to keep them that way. Her job was so high-stress that she told me she wanted our details to remain predictable. She would enter, strip, put on her new panties, and climb me for her orgasms. Then I would take my pleasure of her. We went until either we were out of time or I was out of energy, whichever came first, and then we would cuddle to recuperate during what moments we had remaining. If we had more time than I had vitality, I would paint her nails and listen to her chronicles.

"What is it you see in me?" I asked her during one of our nail-painting sessions. "You clearly outclass me in every way."

She answered, "Because when you rub my feet, you talk about all those teeny little muscles lifting, holding, and balancing me gracefully so my mind can do important work. That's what I see in you, Mark. You think of me as a valuable person inside a body, and you recognize that the two things are separate. This is no small thing to a woman."

We always parted with the same silly ritual when Boulette left: she would lean against the inside of my door while I reapplied her lipstick. It was a ceremony designed to make amends for the damage I had done unto her lips. It was only appropriate, because after trying to lick and suck and pump them off her face, reapplying her lipstick seemed the least I could do for her lips in return.

Most of what I didn't respect about King Fredrick was his inability to concentrate on the real game. It made him lose.

I don't stay in touch with B these days, but I know she's still my dear friend. I include her here in my diary not only because that phase of my life is important to understand regarding my character alterations, but also because B represents something telling about my relationships. I've talked to Pat about it; among the disadvantages of having a one-chapter-at-a-time lifestyle like mine is a lack of relationship carryover, and that pattern is partially responsible for me being the loose cannon that I am today. It's almost as if each affinity is its own short story, and my life is a collection of them without a logline to make sense of it all. It's true that I don't carry enemies forward into my past, but neither do I bring along any friends. Kevin Bruce is my only constant, and even he's a relatively recent arrival. Pity he's not real.

CHAPTER 11

Augean Stables

It seems you can foresee and prophesy beforehand those things which time has not yet shown, but of things present and with you now, you remain uninformed.
—Dante Alighieri, from *The Divine Comedy*, "Inferno," canto X

O ne particular Saturday evening after Frederick's wife left my condo, I went for a drive. Something was up, and I could feel it. The evening air in Louisiana has a way of announcing important events with a feeling on our skin that combines bug-crawls with static electricity, and this was one of those times. I could feel something new abrew. I could feel it coming the same way people fishing on a river can feel a barge approaching just by the way the water swells long before the barge is audible or visible. I was having that feeling. My cosmic river was swelling.

I was in a metacognitive mood when B left, feeling as if I needed to clean up my act and stop having affairs with married women—including Boulette. She had just left me a few hours earlier, and I was satiated. A vice is an easy thing to shed when we're overfull of it. Show me the exit door of an all-you-can-eat buffet, and I'll show you people pledging to go on a weight-loss program, but a diet brochure at the entrance is a waste of paper.

Speaking of restaurants, I was in the mood for some comfort food, so I headed to an Acadian restaurant on Veterans Boulevard where I knew they served excellent poutine. It's common knowledge that Acadians migrated from the Canadian province of Quebec, and poutine is a staple in that area on cold winter days. It warms our bones.

By the way, I once saw something remarkable at this restaurant a few years earlier. I remember it often, and it's too remarkable to not include here in my diary.

I was in the restaurant enjoying my poutine when two punk adolescent kids started giving some discourtesy to the guy behind the counter. His accent was authentic French Quebec Cajun, and the kids were mockingly overarticulating their orders to tease him. Another customer sitting in the shop a few booths from me intervened, and the adolescents started to get aggressive with her in return. The customer reached out in slow motion and touched the boys, telling them she had put a curse on them. She said the curse could be lifted if they apologized to the guy behind the counter. They didn't. In fact, they went to get their parents, who were apparently waiting in a car outside for the boys to return with a take-out order.

When the boys told their parents, they busted out of their car and came into the restaurant to confront the woman. The mother unleashed a string of expletives and slapped the woman's face. Calmly, the woman said to the parents, "Now the curse is also on you, but much more severely." After another explosion of even more expletives, the family stormed out the door without their take-out, putting on quite a show of middle fingers as they departed.

Everyone in the restaurant watched through the window as the car sped out onto Veterans Boulevard. In the blink of an eye, the entire family in that car was killed because the hothead father was too angry to see that he was pulling into the path of an oncoming eighteen-wheeler. Amazingly, the truck driver climbed down out of his rig unscratched. He didn't even limp. Coincidence is coincidence, and one can argue that the wreck was the result of the father's compromised emotional state, not the curse, but the mise-en-scène of that occurrence will forever be too heavy for me to dismiss. In Hebrew scripture, there is no word for "coincidence" because writers believed every situation is from God.

I ate my poutine the Saturday night after B left me, and then I left the restaurant and continued on my drive. My head was swirling, and I reflected on many things. I had only recently started my new career in the barbecue industry at that time, and as these other things churned in my mind, I was also dwelling on a couple of interesting analogies I had freshly learned from the food service industry. For instance, there's a thing called "fajita effect," where the sight, sound, and aroma of a pan of sizzling fajitas being carried through a restaurant creates a cascade of customers ordering fajitas. The phenomenon is real, and experienced kitchen managers brace themselves for the onslaught by preparing additional fajitas as soon as they get the first order. In fact, when the kitchen has a lot of fajita materials to push, or when business is slow, the manager will order the kitchen staff to grill a bunch just to carry it through the restaurant and drum up some hunger. Driving in my car that evening, my sixth sense felt the symbolism of this metaphor, but I couldn't put my mind on exactly how it was happening. I just had a premonition that powerful influences were parading invisible fajitas throughout humanity and that somehow I was supposed to be taking notice of them. Pat watches me intently when I talk like this. So does Obra. And so does Kevin Bruce.

There's one particular auto body shop on Veterans Boulevard that specializes in custom hot rods. The shop is near where the causeway overpass crosses Veterans. Since I was already feeling pouty-pissy, I decided to do some window-shopping and let my poutine settle. Such had become my lifestyle: dating other men's wives, and window-shopping. I parked in the lot beside the showroom and walked to the glass. The shop had already closed for the day. I tried not to leave face smudges on the glass like a kid at a candy store.

There's a bus stop on the corner by the shop. That's where I first saw the woman. I saw her reflection, ghostlike, beside mine on the showroom glass. The optical illusion was that she actually stood beside me. The woman looked familiar, but I couldn't quite place where I had seen her before.

Something about the behavior of the woman at the bus stop made my brain notice her even though my mind wanted to be left alone. She wasn't just close to me; her nearness involved me, and that's the thing that attracted my attention. It wasn't just the hair choreography she flipped or the sexy back-sway to her posture I noticed; it was that I felt she wanted to be on my radar. I sensed that she wanted me around, but she didn't want to be bothered by me; and she wanted me within reach, but she didn't really care about me. Without turning my head, I studied her reflection in the window. I was trying to remember where I had seen her.

There was something spooky about seeing the ghostly reflection of this woman floating on the glass between me and the cars. Even in the reflection, I could see a lot of details about her. Her hair was thick and shiny, and that usually means a quality lifestyle. Specifically, it means money. I could tell that she ordinarily put on quite a visual performance, but for now, this woman just looked tired and jumpy—in spite of her big-money hair. She didn't talk to me or look at me at first. She just stood there, keeping me within range and nervously glancing around us.

She was kind of pretty but not my type. She was a little too leggy and blond for my tastes. She had sharp, Northern European features and high-dollar clothes. She would have been beautiful if not for her barnyard-cat countenance. Even an attractive face like hers can't overcome go-to-hell eyes. She had an air of store-bought classiness, and I wondered why she was at a city bus stop. Women who look that upper-crust usually don't take the bus.

She didn't exactly have the persona of a prostitute, but at the same time, she kind of did. She didn't seem to be a professional out-and-out prostitute, anyway. Maybe she was just a B-girl getting off work.

Strumpet or not, this woman had clearly been recently well sexed. I knew this because I was an exemplar of the look people develop when we get good at rushing out of bed and throwing our image together so we can hurry out into public. In spite of her obvious attempts at beau monde carriage, this woman was reeking of that skill. It was among the reasons why I wanted no part of her. Bloodsuckers usually avoid each other, especially the pretty ones like us. Besides, I'm not inclined to share a bad day with people I don't know, particularly if it wasn't my bad day to start with. I made myself look away from her reflection and tried to forget she was there. She must have sensed this, because she moved closer to me.

"A girl can tell a lot about how a guy treats women just by the way he looks at cars," she said to me out of the blue. She didn't have a chance to elaborate, because just then, in the midst of my suspicion, a car pulled quickly to the curb. It came in hot and skidded a little sideways as it came to a stop.

The woman walked toward me briskly, keeping her eyes on the car as she did it. She must have had a gravitational knowledge of where I was, because even though she wasn't looking at me, she came straight to me. A man hopped out of the car and trotted toward us, and she quickened her pace toward me. He looked familiar, too, but I didn't have time to dwell on that because they were both coming at me fast. Thinking that I was about to be mugged, I readied myself to snap-kick the first one and roundhouse the second one, but it didn't go that way.

"Get in the car!" the man said to the woman. He didn't appear to even see me. He wasn't fully yelling at her, but he wasn't just talking either. He meant business. I didn't know what this woman had done to the guy, but it must have been something awful.

"Brute ..." was her only reply. It was an odd thing to say, especially the way she said it—calm and with a strange combination of pejorative and nickname. It was cartoonish and a little archaic. She said it childlike, as if there was more she wanted to add but she couldn't concentrate long enough to find the next words. She moved closer to me.

"Get in the car!"

"Brute ..."

"Get in the car."

"Brute, leave me alone!"

"Get in the car!"

"Leave me alone!"

All in all, I guess they repeated those two sentences about four times before he finally put his hands on her. He didn't really hit her, but the clutch was certainly more forceful than needed. Even though I didn't know her or care about her, I took umbrage at his intensity. My first instinct tends to be chivalrous. It's a ruinous characteristic.

The instant his hands started moving at her, she leaped toward me. The man and I grappled for the woman.

Things were surreal at first. He was tugging on her and saying, "Come on!" and she was holding on to me. I had a grip on her jacket as I pulled, and I tried to talk to the guy.

"Come on, man," I softly said. I repeated the words several times, cucumber cool.

I consider it odd that until now, as I see these words in writing for the first time, I never realized I was saying almost the same thing he was saying, except that he was saying exactly what he meant, and I was saying exactly the opposite.

The woman wasn't fighting—I think she saw me as the one who should do that—but she was resisting, and I felt an instinct to assist her. It had to be instinct because if I had taken only a moment to think about it, I would have walked away and let them kick the shit out of each other.

After unsuccessfully trying to talk to him, the woman started talking to me. She was showing me bruises as quickly as she could. She clutched me with one hand while she pulled her clothes away from her neck with the other to show me the marks on her throat and shoulders. She even managed to pull her jacket up over her ribs to show me a few bruises there. It's amazing how much she showed me, one-handed and in the midst of all that tussle.

The man didn't address me directly for five or six seconds, but that time felt like a day or two of wrestling over the woman. I guess he grew tired of me, because he stopped tugging on the woman and looked me straight in the face.

"You don't even want to get into this!" he said. He was right, but really, what were my options? My mind screamed, "No shit, Sherlock!" but my mouth soothingly said, "Come on, man."

I guess rationality broke through to the guy's brain, because he let go and stepped back. For the first time since the incident started, there was intelligence in his eyes. He appeared to be actually thinking, and it was an important development. It felt as though he saw what he was doing and couldn't believe it.

"I'm outta here!" he proclaimed, symbolically gesturing with his hands angrily down toward the ground as if he had thrown something vile away from him. He turned to leave. He was departing, and the incident was over. It was the perfect three-act play: setup, conflict, and resolution. The curtain was dropping, and the audience was about to applaud.

There is no peace as intense as that which comes after a storm. This is a fact, and it is one of the few truly beautiful moments life ever gives us. The longer the winter, the better the spring. Unfortunately, since our bug-tussle lasted less than a half minute, this particular spring was pretty damn short. Reconciliation had indeed found us, but the froward woman wouldn't leave it that way.

"Yeah, run away like the coward you are!" the woman impugned at the back of the poor bastard's departing head. "Now that there's a real man here, all you do is tuck tail and run!"

I wanted to kill her, and I don't mean that symbolically. I didn't even know her, yet here she was dragging me into her sepia. Again!

The man physically jolted when her rabbit-punch insults hit him. He stopped and slowly turned in his tracks. I looked at his eyes, and all the intelligence I had seen there only a moment before was gone. As triumvirates go, this one was going to suck.

It took the man two seconds to reach us, and it took the woman even less than that to get on the other side of me. She was climbing on my back and spider-monkey screeching. She was also clutching at my arms, which wasn't helping me win the fight.

I know the woman was panicking, and I try to be sympathetic with people when they're emotional. I also know that she shouldn't be held in strict accountability, given what she was going through, and I know it's hard to be at our best under a shower of fists, but I swear that, a couple of times, it seemed she was restraining me and protecting this guy. I think she wanted him to get his ass kicked, but she didn't want him to get hurt.

I don't know who would have won or lost that fight, but what with the princess climbing on me and screaming in my ear and blocking my vision and getting in my way, I wasn't feeling all that optimistic. The guy was landing a few good blows, and in addition to feeling an aching in my muscles and a burning in my lungs, I was starting to feel the effects of his punches. I remember landing a couple of good right crosses into his face and several uppercuts into his ribs, but I felt slipshod. I was out of practice.

I'm glad I was in good shape. The best defense is stamina. I must have been causing him some pain, because the next thing I knew, he jumped back and threw his hands into the air as a gesture of withdrawal, and he eased back from the fight. My pride would like me to feel that I beat him away, but in fact, I think he just grew weary of the whole affair. The look on his face said this woman was worth a squabble but not a full-fledged, whoop-ass fight.

The man took a few guarded steps backward, and as he recognized that I wasn't interested in pursuing him, he turned to walk away. The woman unraveled herself from around me as she climbed down, and then she pulled her fingernails out of my clothing and came out from behind me to run and jump on the guy. She apparently had a disease that prevented her from knowing when to quit. I, being of sound mind and dull disposition, know perfectly well when to quit and how to do it. These abilities are what make me lose most of my battles yet win all my wars.

After she jumped on the man's back, the woman slapped him and scratched him and pulled his hair and yelled at him. She was good at it. I think she warmed up by practicing on me.

After a couple of seconds, the man had a chance to peel her off and pop her in the face a few times. Specifically, it was three times, and each blow was a powerful, long-armed, full-fisted punch that smashed her straight and deep in the lips. Blood splattered everywhere.

As ensanguined as she was, I didn't move a muscle to assist her this time. You haven't lived until you've seen someone who infuriates you get punched three full-forced times in the mouth. It bears repeating that I know when to quit, and I was not about to interfere on her behalf again.

After he hit her those three times, the man stepped back, turned kind of slowly, and walked away. Peace had been restored to the universe once again.

She wobbled on her feet for a couple of seconds after he turned away, and then the woman's legs melted. Her entire body collapsed in a pile from the bottom up like a rope loosed from a ladder.

My adrenaline was wearing off, and my aches were arriving, so I turned and started walking toward my car. I knew I needed to get in my car and start driving right away, because I wanted to be safe at another location when the tremors set in. I was intentionally *ujjayi-breathing* because I knew very well I was starting to show the early symptoms of shock. I wanted to drive while my head was clear. I had been through shock-inducing events before, and if I was going to get feeble in the aftermath of this one, I wanted to be someplace else when it happened.

The guy had jumped into his car by then and was speeding his way into the flow of traffic on Veterans Boulevard. I was glad to see him go. During the fight, about fifty cars passed us, but not one of them stopped. I don't blame them. One should not disrupt a perfectly good drive to participate in other people's truculence.

I crawled into my own car and leaned back against the headrest. After a few seconds of deep breathing and psychological recovery, I started my car and put it in gear. I was ready to leave, but then I looked out of my car window to check on the woman. She was trying to get up but was still woozy.

I don't know what made me do it, but with a sigh of self-exasperation I crawled back out of my car and made my way slowly to her. With each step, I amazed even myself. She wasn't trying to stand any more when I reached her. She was just sitting there on the pavement, clearly still dazed. As I helped her to her feet, she just kept barking, "See what I mean! Did you see him hit me?"

I didn't answer. A woman like that will get you killed, and other than saving her from herself, I wanted no part of her. I just wanted get her to safety and leave—that's all.

I took the woman to my car, half slinging her and half assisting her. I leaned her against the side of the car and pulled a blanket out of the trunk and wrapped it around her to keep her warm—and to keep her blood and goo off of my car seat. If you're wondering why I had a blanket in my car, just remember that I was a bachelor—an active and talented one.

As I pushed her into the passenger door and put the blanket and seatbelt around her, I kept telling the woman that we should leave immediately, just in case the guy came back with a gun or something. She nodded in agreement. It seemed she hadn't thought of that before. I was partially talking to her and partially just talking to keep my brain focused. I trotted around the car and climbed behind the steering wheel as quickly as I could.

We drove only a few blocks before she asked to be let out. I was surprised. Counting the time spent at red lights and all, a few minutes had passed, but we hadn't gone far.

I pulled the car around the next corner and up to the curb, then stopped. I looked around to be sure we weren't being followed, then put the car in park but left the motor running.

The woman had mostly recovered, but her mood swung between crying and laughing in a way that worried me. My concerns were unfounded, because it turns out she has pseudobulbar affect, mostly triggered by riding in a car in traffic. Her behavior had nothing to do with getting the shit beat out of her. Can you imagine the irony?

As we sat at the curb, the woman cleaned her face a little with some napkins from my glove compartment. She wasn't crying or laughing anymore, and she didn't look much different than when I first saw her at the bus stop. In fact, except for slightly swollen lips, she looked almost exactly the same. I thought it was remarkable, but I recognize the significance. The fight might have been an extraordinary event for me, but it was just another day in her life. I was in war mode, but she thought it was just another argument.

We all have a comfort zone, and this woman had a very large one, much larger than mine, which is significant because my comfort zone had grown pretty dang big in those days. Seeing her ability to recuperate in the space of a sizzle reel made me realize why she handled the confrontation so incautiously. She didn't care if it continued, and she was secure within herself no matter how the fight ended. However it went, she would be unaltered. It sunk into me again what a judgmental, cowardly bastard I can be.

"Where have I seen you before?" I heard myself ask. She stopped cleaning her face with the napkin and looked at me; then she snickered, shook her head, and returned to her task without answering.

She asked me if I would be a witness for her just in case he did her any more damage, and, like the dumbass I am, I agreed. As we exchanged contact information, she asked me not to call the press. I agreed, but I thought it was an odd request. I was much more likely to call the police than the press. Wouldn't normal people do that?

Who is she? I wondered. I looked at the piece of paper and saw that she had written her name and what I guessed was the name of the guy who punched her. The names seemed familiar, but I couldn't place them.

"You don't have to live like this," I said as I read her note. The tone in my voice was a little accusatory and condescending. Maybe even proscribed. I looked at her and immediately regretted giving her advice. She turned her face at me. The "up yours" look in her eyes was enough castigation to stop my sanguine, uninvited advice. I felt immediately guilty for the barnyard-cat comparisons I conjured up when I first saw her at the bus stop. Barnyard cats are as tough as nails, and weaklings like me should admire them, not judge them.

"Look," she said, "if you want honor among thieves, then you'd better hang out with people who steal for sport. The rest of us have a life to sustain, and sustenance can get ugly. It's tough to be uncompromised when your mortgage is linked to your choices." Her comeback was exculpatory.

I continued to look at the woman, but slowly. Compared to the insight of her philosopher's stone, I had nothing but tailgate-party sagacity to offer, so I remained quiet. She knew a lot more than I knew, and compared to her, I had a coward's track record of victories over soft targets. I think she saw that realization in me, because she smiled slightly, mostly with her eyes. It was the look of someone who had just been vindicated, and I think for the first time since we met, she liked me.

"Is there anything I can do for you?" I asked after a while. Our conversation was clearly coming to an end.

"No. Just let it go."

"Let it go? How can you say that?" I was genuinely interested in what her reply would be, and I think it showed.

She studied me patiently, but she also had the look of someone who was clearly finished with something. It felt as though she was trying to decide between speaking and shrugging her shoulders. She stayed that way for the space of a breath or two.

"Don't swing your flyswatter so hard, pal," she coolly said after her pause. "A simple flick of the wrist will do." She hesitated and stared vacuously ahead as if something big had just occurred to her. "Wound the flies so they fall to the ground where ants can reach them, then let the ants do the killing." She added the last part in a half voice, almost mumbling to herself. I had a feeling there was fly-swatting and ant-feeding in her future.

She patted me on the arm with her left hand and opened the car door with her right, doing each thing smoothly and simultaneously. Then, just like that, she slipped out of my car. She stood up, turned around, and leaned into the door to face me for just a moment. "You were great," she said. She closed the door and walked gracefully away. I watched her until she left the last streetlight behind and darkness swallowed her.

CHAPTER 12

WYSIWYG Wisdom

That wretch up there which has the greatest punishment is Judas
Iscariot. As for the other two, they are Brutus and Cassius.
—Dante Alighieri, from *The Divine Comedy*, "Inferno," canto XXXIV

The woman at the bus stop had a name. It was Cass. She was the queen of the Stockholm syndrome, which made her dangerous—even to herself. The way the syndrome worked for Cass is that the worse a man treated her, the more she had to have him in her life. She demonstrated that behavior right in front of me with Brute in the first three minutes we met. When he retreated, she dug her claws into him. Cass had the capacity to be a dedicated partner, but she needed to get dumped every day in order for that to happen.

By the way, the reason Cass looked familiar to me is that she's on the city council. So is Brute, the guy who attacked her. I don't trust politicians, so I didn't spend time with any of them in person. That said, it's not likely I would recognize either Cass or Brute outside of television, and particularly not within the circumstances where we met. Incidentally, they've both become infamous since then— bywords for betrayal.

As for me, I've always been safe from women like Cass because I don't know how to treat a woman badly. I treat women with a slow kind of respect, and it drives the evil ones away. Respect and prudence to a chubi are like daylight and garlic to a vampire.

After Cass stepped out of my car that Saturday night, I went home. She called early Sunday morning. I was awake, but it wasn't because I was up already; it was because I was up still. I really wasn't all that enthusiastic to hear from her, which had the bastardized effect of drawing her to me. Cass wasn't familiar with lukewarm receptions from men, so my lack of enthusiasm was metal to her magnet.

I thought Cass was calling only to give me an update on the fight. After she gave me this news, I expected her to hang up. She didn't. What a dense bastard I can be. We talked for a while. That's when she told me she and the guy were on the city council.

Cass was persistent. She called a lot after that. She made me laugh.

I spontaneously asked her one day on the phone, "Which superpower would you like to have?"

"Redolence," she said without so much as a second's hesitation. Apparently she had given the matter some previous thought. "I want to be Aroma Girl, the woman who smells wonderful and gives off a powerful, persuasive fragrance."

After a dumbfounded momentary pause, I prodded, "That's your superpower?"

"Yep."

"You don't want to fly or become invisible or read minds … you just want to smell wonderful?"

"Yep."

"That's how you're going to waste a chance to acquire a superpower?"

"It's not a waste—it's an investment."

Cass may have been a nuisance, but she was charming. She was also wise, so even now I try to not second-guess her desire to be redolent.

Hearing Cass say these things was interesting, and it also helped me understand why she tended to make trouble out of peace. A smart cat can learn a lot of things by watching other cats jump onto stoves, and Cass was that kind of cat. She was also the kind that prods other cats into jumping first so they can be the ones that test the heat of the stove, which is what gave me so much pause about her. Even at the height of our relationship, I kept her at arm's length.

We talked every day when I came home from work, and she would usually call again the next morning to awaken me, which I enjoyed a whole lot better than the sound of my alarm. I still didn't want her too close, because I didn't trust her, yet neither did I want her to stop giving me attention. Looking back, I think her approach to relationships was rubbing off on me.

Cass was puzzled when I proved immune to her allure. The truth is, she just wasn't my type. As I wrote before, she was too skinny and blond for me. I need to document here that I never had sex with Cass. At first this was because I was having sex with several other women, and adding her to the list would only have complicated my life in pointless ways, but after a while, it was because I wasn't having sex with anyone—but that's another story. Let's just say I had entered a point in my life where I wasn't likely to suffer any romance-related injuries.

In every relationship, the person who is the most cavalier is the one who ends up with the most control. Other than liking the attention she gave me, I couldn't have had less of a care about Cass, and that put me in charge. I understood her, which kept me safe. I'm low on the drama meter, so Cass finds me when her ship is listing and she wants ballast and stability, but as soon as she gets bored with our superficiality, she wanders off again. I'm good with that.

By the way, "Cass" is an abbreviation of her real name. I asked her once why she didn't use her full name, and she told me it was a man's name and it was so ancient that it sounded funny. About three seconds later, I guessed her name.

Cass was surprised I guessed her name so quickly. It was not a challenging achievement for me. I'm a fan of literary classics, particularly from the Mediterranean basin. Besides, the name fit her.

I guess you just have to be in a relationship with a person like Cass to know what it is to be fond of someone you don't trust. She has a lean and hungry look. She thinks too much, and it is well documented in the world's best literature that such people are dangerous.

Cass is devoted to public service, which is admirable, but she loves it because of the profile, not the people. She wants nothing more than to be famous for saving an orphanage from the Frankenstein monster, which is also admirable—except that void of a monster, she's prone to invent one. That's what makes her untrustworthy. Those two things. She believes her own hype, and she manufactures Frankenstein monsters as needed.

Inventing problems for the purpose of solving them later isn't limited to politicians. In fact, the behavior is so common that it has a name: firefighter arson syndrome. I've only recently learned of the term, and when I did my mind went straight to Cass.

Toward the end of our interaction, Cass's mood grew darker. Something was happening. When I first met her, she was mostly light and occasionally dark, but toward the end, that ratio reversed, so much so that I quit trying to cheer her gloomy disposition.

"Listen to me boy, and hear me good!" she barked during one of our very last conversations. "Good leaders never let harm come to their followers, but great leaders know to let the train wreck every once in a while. People love us when they need us, but they hate us when they're comfortable."

Cass and I didn't have a lot to say after that. My values are too old-world to poison the well simply for the sake of winning, so I put some distance between us. Maybe I'm simple. And a little lazy.

We soon moved on—I to my deeds, and Cass to hers. I was polite to Cass after that, but I never showed her any weakness. Emotional boundaries make functional relationships in the same way that good fences make good neighbors.

Cass is symbolic of the life I had made for myself. My life was moneyed but not better. My whores wore diamonds and my enemies smiled at me, but they were still whores and enemies. Treachery is a powerful thing.

CHAPTER 13

Kibroth Hattaavah

He who brought the rest to play the fool was angriest.
Mischief extreme—meant only to procure more woe.
—Dante Alighieri, from *The Divine Comedy*, "Inferno," canto XXI

Owning my own barbecue business was lot of work. In fact, I worked just about all the time, but the schedule was flexible, and that made the long hours sustainable.

In the first phase of my business, I cooked for gatherings of all types: church outings, school field trips, sorority and fraternity functions, company picnics, family reunions, Elks gatherings. If you had some money and a group of hungry people, I had a towable barbecue grill.

After a while, I refined my business. I built a bigger smoker. I also had a more selective clientele and a more sophisticated menu. I sold the Joe Barbecue business and then used the money to start another catering service named Dr. Croupier Amity. I still had an alfresco niche, but I didn't flip burgers for just any old party. I prepared elaborate patio-style meals, soup-to-nuts, for very special "friends."

By the concluding months of that phase, the gatherings were small—very small. Profits were high—very high. I made a lot of money when I sold Joe Barbecue, and I had the good sense to spin it into my future.

The "special friends" portion of my barbecue business was the middle phase. At the end of that phase, I entered the third—and final—phase. It was the most lucrative of all. The gatherings for the Joe Barbecue phase were large and gainful, and the gatherings for the Dr. Croupier Amity phase were smaller and even more profitable, so continuing with the trend, the gatherings for the third phase were tiny and downright fructiferous. I sold Dr. Croupier Amity and spun the equity into a new cooking business called Zero Risk Bias. The only kind of cooking I did during that phase was for occasions of extreme secrecy and betrayal. Mostly, I cooked for couples who were married, but not to each other. Occasionally there were covert business mergers, but not many. During this new phase of my business, my client list was pretty much restricted to just cooking for dalliance. I had devolved into being that kind of business owner.

Through personal experience, I had become an expert in the nuance of extramarital affairs, and I was familiar with how they create a glowing aura of something special alighting upon us. It gives us the feeling we're immune and makes us believe we have outsmarted the entire world. Adulterers think they're playing hide-and-seek when they're in that mood, but everyone else sees show-and-tell. It's a hormone-infected, grass-is-greener syndrome come true, and in the throes of this adrenaline-fueled bliss, the more we pay, the better we feel. It's pure craziness. People are willing to pay a grossly overpriced fee for being doted upon when in that frame of mind, and I charged in a way that was commensurate with the attitudinal euphoria of my clients.

There are sierras of Freudian things going on inside people's heads during periods of extramarital dalliance, and I took them all the way to the bank. It's easy to confuse gliding with cascading as long as we're airborne, but nobody is ever confused during the landing.

Word spread that I was a man who could provide a service and keep a secret. The events were so expensive that I had only serious clients. I intentionally didn't cook more often than every two weeks or so. I didn't want my clients' paths to cross.

I didn't like the seraglio aspect of my Zero Risk Bias phase of business, but I did enjoy the menu and the money. In a way, I was proud of the high quality of what I did, but in another way, not so much. If karma had come to me in those days and said, "You're going to get what you do times ten," I wouldn't have known whether to be elated or panicked.

Every job rubs a sore spot on us somewhere. Sometimes it's a physical welt, and sometimes it's emotional. We can't do something over and over and over again without suffering some kind of repetitive-motion injury, visible or not. Sometimes it's our very lifestyle that gives us a blister. My sore spot was coming from the cover-up. At that point, I realized I was becoming a high-dollar ergate. I had become a respectable loon, and if I wanted to keep my dignity, I had to stop. I was the common denominator in too many ignominious combinations, and it was getting hard for me to keep a poker face. That kind of circumstance cannot help but end badly if we remain too long within it.

Some people don't care what they do for a living as long as the paycheck doesn't bounce, but I'm not like that. I have to understand the gestalt and value of what I'm doing, and I need to create something lasting. I guess that's the difference between an entrepreneur and an artist.

CHAPTER 14

Ne Plus Ultra

Are you aware that he who comes behind moves with
his feet? The feet of the dead are not so used.
He is indeed alive, so on his lonely quest I must lead him through the
vales of night. Necessity brings him here, not delight or sport.
—Dante Alighieri, from *The Divine Comedy*, "Inferno," canto XII

L uckily, Fate took care of me during the entrepreneurial phase of my life, and I made a ton of money. I also met a lot of rich, powerful people. I learned from them—mostly that longstanding success requires three things: the backbone to do something, the fortitude to keep your mouth shut when necessary, and the sense to not partner with gastropods, because they'll leave a slime trail you can't cover. It seems like this third point should be obvious, but it turns out it's the one that keeps most people from accumulating wealth. Considering my history, I have avoided that pitfall. Divine guidance, I guess. Or Kevin Bruce, the poor bastard.

Those three guidelines made me successful in a lot of ways, not just financially—especially later, when I worked in the Club. Those details will have to wait.

Contrary to popular assumptions, not all rich and powerful people like to be excluded from the kitchen, even if the kitchen isn't a real kitchen at all. In fact, about half the time, the biggest and best among my clients visited with me about simple topics while I cooked. There's something exclusive about being invited into "the kitchen." It's like a backstage pass. I fed my most important clients samples straight off the grill. While they were standing there, they customized the recipe and directed the show. It was empowering for them. They also gave me business advice, which endorses both the mentor and the protégé.

During the final months of my food industry career, I developed an event called a "pull," as in, "Come to a pull at my house tonight." Having a pull became trendy. I increased my fortune tremendously. In fact, the very word "pull" lasts even yet for dining events where the food and the dialogue are of equal importance.

Imagine that—me contributing to the lexicon of culinology. A pull emphasizes interaction and eating equally, and on a simpler level, it gives people something to do with their hands during those damn-awkward pauses in the conversation. The name "pull" comes from the act of pulling cooked meat apart with your bare hands and eating it without utensils. It's a valence of the product and the event. The preparation is to cook an entire animal and put it on a table so people can stand around the edges, pulling the meat apart and putting it on their plates with other kinds of hand-eaten food. It's kind of like combining a traditional Cajun boucherie with a South African braai. It's messy, but that's half the fun. It's also primitive, and that's the other half of the fun. It's as bougie as an alfresco dining event can be. There's nothing refined about a pull, yet there's something erotic and aphrodisiac about it. I think New Orleans had a baby boom that next year.

Occasionally, I still overhear people talking about having a pull. It smacks my pride a little when people say the word in my presence, because they have no idea that I'm the inventor of the craze, but such has always been the invisible quality of my life.

Pulls were trendy, so naturally they were short-lived. They got so popular that I made a fortune through a spin-off business selling ingredients and renting equipment for pulls that other people would cook: firewood, cast-iron pots and tripods, seasoning, and logo-branded tablecloths that were hefty enough to sustain the abuse. I even marketed a recipe for a marinade that had to sit on your kitchen counter for a week before you used it, and watching it brew was part of the fun of anticipating your very own custom pull.

Suddenly it was all yesterday's news. No one was doing it any more—at least not nearly to the extent that pulls once enjoyed. Having gone from zeitgeist to bygone overnight, I sold the business.

I was "R-I-C-H" rich! No sunk cost fallacy for me; I moved on.

CHAPTER 15

Phinehas Meets Zimri and Cozbi

Then my mentor said, "In order that you may comprehend this ring, go forward so that you can view these shades and learn their state, but do not parley long in discourse among them, lest you waste our time and succumb to their ways."
—Dante Alighieri, from *The Divine Comedy*, "Inferno," canto XVII

One particular guy I met during the restaurant phase of my life had a big, handsome house and a beautiful wife with big, beautiful breasts. His last name was Zecue. The name probably sounds familiar because the Zecue family is well known in New Orleans.

The guy's first name was Bell. Before you judge his parents too harshly for giving a kid a name like Bell Zecue, let me say it was a nickname he earned through street credibility.

I met Bell through a friend of a friend during lunch at one of those old New Orleans restaurants that have been around for so long that people use them as landmarks. The restaurant is called Castello Angelo's. The address is 1300 Boniface Drive, on the edge of Cocytus Bay, right about where Styx River enters Lake Pontchartrain.

That day at lunch, Bell, being the perfect host, invited me to a party at his house. I, being the perfect guest, accepted.

As I described Bell a few paragraphs ago, I felt a need to mention his big house and his beautiful wife and her big breasts because they were all so emblematic to his *luxe et volupté* identity that they can't be left out of his portrait. I liked being at the parties at Bell's big house.

I also liked his wife and her big breasts. I enjoyed them. She enjoyed me enjoying them.

I don't think Bell knew anything about that last part, but I could be mistaken. Empires are built by people who don't have standard values. Just because Bell didn't kill me for familiarizing myself with his wife's hooters doesn't mean he didn't know what I was doing with them.

Bell's wife told me once that having large breasts was a curse of riches. They made her life easy in a lot of trivial ways but hindered her with the important things and cursed her with an anterior destiny.

"I can get a cab on a crowded street faster than anyone else," she said to me one day, "and I can get really good service in gas stations and restaurants." We were lying on our backs on the carpet in Bell's study. "I can do these kinds of little things, but I can't be taken seriously at work. That's why I quit. Everybody thinks I quit working because I married Bell, but that's not the reason. I quit because my boobs make it hard for people to respect my job performance. Big boobs open doors for women, but they also keep us from moving beyond the threshold."

I thought it was an insightful conundrum. I guess we all have our own curse of riches in some way or another. Hers curse is just more obvious.

"I can't find pretty clothes to fit my chesty little body, I get neck pains and tension headaches from constantly having to pull myself backward, and I'm pretty much relegated to sleeping on my back for the rest of my life. And growing up is tough for busty girls; it sucks to be any girl growing up, no matter who she is, but it's especially hard for young girls who have big boobs."

"Were you molested as a child?" I asked. I turned my face to her on the carpeting as I asked her the question. She looked silently at the ceiling for a pause before answering.

"Yes—I had boobs before I had brains, so how could it go any other way? It's a wonder I like men at all." She said the words matter-of-factly, half whispered in an almost trancelike state of resignation.

There was a trace of remorse in her reply, but I did not hear any bitterness.

"Did you report it?"

"No."

"Can I ask why not?"

"It's complicated," she whispered, rolling her head away from me on the carpeting. I decided to hear her but not ask any more questions.

"I didn't report it because news like that never comes out without everyone getting messy, even the victim," she said. "I mean, there's the whole 'used furniture' thing, and I didn't want to be seen as damaged goods among the kids at school. I didn't want boys thinking that since I was experienced I would be easy. Even people's support makes it worse for girls who talk. Do-gooders make it sound so simple, so black-and-white, but it's not. There's plenty of blame and dirt for everyone, and that's part of what makes victims feel bad. People act like we should be all militant and angry, hating the men who did it, but if that's not how we feel, we start to question ourselves ... our own worth." She paused and turned her face to me. "Know what I mean?" The question wasn't rhetorical, so I answered.

"Not from firsthand experience," I softly replied. "I don't have any experience with sexual molestation from any angle. I don't even think it happened in my family. With me it was punches, not sex."

"I could tell that about you." She said the words caringly, and I appreciated her for it.

"Do you feel harassed as an adult?" I asked.

"Not after I married Bell," she replied, "but before that, yes, quite a lot."

"What did you do about it?"

"Nothing. Not a thing."

"I'm curious to know why. Am I being too intrusive?"

She hesitated and then said, "We women have warning signs at first, but we aren't always in a position to do anything about it, so we push ahead. Sometimes we love the man, sometimes we need the job—there are a lot of things that keep us quiet. Every woman is a

Kassandra that way, blessed with insight but cursed with an inability to make anyone understand." She paused for a moment and then continued. "After a while, I got used to it, I guess. Or I considered it a toll I had to pay before I could cross the bridges in my life … in my development. Mixed in with all that is a little self-doubt and probably a lot of other emotions. Like I said, it's complicated."

"Ironic that your name is Cassandra."

"I know, right? That's how I found the metaphor. But I spell it with a *C*."

Then she looked straight at me, hard. "What did you do about being beaten?" she asked.

"Nothing. Not a thing," I said. "Big boys don't cry. Besides, I wasn't really beaten, just smacked around a lot. People like me always surrender too early to get a serious mauling."

"You don't think highly of yourself, do you Mark?"

"It comes and goes," I replied.

After a pause of just looking at me, she said, "Seriously, why didn't you say anything?"

I hesitated to think and then said, "It was all around me, so I thought it was just one of life's circumstances—kind of like I was supposed to be able to live with it, and complaining would have meant I was weaker and inferior."

"Weaker and inferior to what?"

"Normalcy" was my answer.

"It's odd that someone with such a low self-image would be so strong, responsible, and honorable," Cassandra said.

"Yep, that's me all over—odd, strong, responsible, and honorable." She giggled a little.

"Did you ever abuse a child?" she asked. As before, she said these words softly and lovingly, as though she was trying to help me understand something buried deep within myself.

"No. I never even created a situation when it could have occurred. I'll die before I injure a child. Why do you ask?"

"Because a lot of abused children grow up to be abusers themselves," she said, "and I was wondering if that's why you feel so poorly about yourself."

I thought about her observation silently for a half minute and then said, "Being abused or bullied can make us sympathetic as much as it can make us vengeful. I'm more likely to protect a kid than to injure one. I grew like a weed as an adolescent, so I outpaced my physical vulnerability. Maybe other victims didn't have that chance, so it's harder now for them to be kind as adults."

I listened to Cassandra earnestly not only on that day, but on all other days as well. I believed that she was smart, and I respected her and ogled her and massaged her and flirted with her and teased her and made her laugh and reminded her that she was beautiful and brainy, but I didn't affect her life one bit. Relationships like that are fun, but they don't go anywhere, and I was yearning to build a life with meaning. Pat is going to have a field day with this information. I'll blame it on Kevin Bruce.

I'm reflecting on this in such detail now because my physical relationship with Bell's wife ended abruptly. It ended because of something she said as we were walking out of Bell's study the day we were lying on the carpet. It wasn't an intentional insult or anything like that, but it cut me. Deeply. It made me feel insignificant. Her words lasted no more than an instant, but that instant was a lapidary moment for me, carved in stone for the rest of my life. I cannot overstate the impact of how what she said changed the rest of my life.

What happened is that, as we were leaving Bell's study, I noticed we left a snow-angel kind of imprint on the carpet where we were lying during our conversation. I mentioned it to Cassandra.

"Don't worry," she said playfully, touching my arm as she spoke, "the maid will soon sweep away all trace of you, and no one will ever know you were even here."

All the king's horses and all the king's men couldn't remove Bell's mark on the world, no matter how hard they tried, yet a charwoman with a vacuum cleaner performing her normal everyday duties could sweep away my hallmark without even paying attention to what she had done. It was that realization—not fear, guilt, or morality—that told me I needed to keep my nickel-and-dime hands off Bell's wife.

After that, I visited with Bell but did not spend any more alone time with his wife. The transition was easy because I genuinely liked Bell. I still do. Very much.

When I first met Bell at the restaurant, he immediately gave me advice. I didn't like when he did that, but in fairness to him, I should say there's something about me that inspires uninvited counsel. It happens all the time, or at least it did back in those days.

Even though I didn't like the presumption with which he gave me counsel, I took Bell's advice, and I benefitted. In exchange for that, I did him a favor. At least that's part of why I did Bell the favor. The other part is a silent apology for fondling his wife.

What happened is I had an opportunity to swat one of Bell's enemies. The guy's name was Riner Salse. Bell vented openly to his friends about his enemies, and I remember him specifically mentioning this one. The only thought I gave to Riner Salse at the time was why someone of Bell's status ever noticed him in the first place.

Through the grapevine, I learned that Salse was going to commit a crime. Peccant people require quite a bit of talking before they can do anything, so Salse talked about his plans. He talked too much, so it's not really coincidental that I learned about what he said. The only coincidental thing is that my friend, Bell, hated this guy, so I paid attention to what I heard.

The crime was nothing spectacular. As I said, Riner Salse was small-time. He was going to steal some money and guns from a gas station / sporting goods store / juke joint in a hick, Podunk burg just to the northeast of New Orleans. He'd already spent time in prison and proclaimed he'd rather die than go back—at least those are the comments he made. It's the public announcement that was important, because that's the part I could use.

Not long after I heard that news, I was at Bell's house, and we were talking alone on the deck in his backyard—scotch in one hand, and cigars in the other. He was conversationally yammering on about

Riner Salse, and I asked him if he would like it if the guy got killed. Like most know-it-alls, Bell thought there was nothing more to me than what he directly observed, so he dismissively laughed. He was wrong.

Bell noticed I was serious, and he eventually stopped chuckling. I said I wouldn't tell him all the details of my plan, but I told him that no matter how natural or coincidental it looked, and no matter what the media had to say about the cause of his death, if Riner Salse died soon, then I was the one who did it, and I did it for him.

"Okay," was all Bell said. He said it with a shrug, which is the Cosa Nostra version of a poker face.

I smirk a little now when I look back at the thin plans I designed to get rid of Salse. I think my recent experience with Andrea, Obra, and Geryon had made me a little cocky about danger, so I organized this event on the fly. My work with Obra went off without a hitch, so as I planned this adventure, I think I skimmed through some important details. It's that second time that gets us into trouble—the one that's between being careful and being adept. A little knowledge is a dangerous thing.

The plan was this: I have a friend who works as a police officer, and she works in the general area of where Salse was going to attempt his robbery, so I set up a scenario wherein she would kill him during the attempted robbery. At the time, my friend was new to the police force, and she needed some recognition. She's a good person, honestly ready to protect and serve, and I wanted to help her get some favorable media. I thought that if she intervened in the process of Salse breaking into the store, then she could get recognition, and Salse would get killed in the process of resisting arrest.

I've known my friend, the police officer, for a few years now. Her name is Ghisola Thibault. Her real first name is Ghisolabella, but even she can't live up to a name with that many syllables, so everybody just calls her Ghisola.

In addition to her delightful sarcasm, our friendship started because Ghisola is a hunter and dog enthusiast like me. I didn't own any dogs at the time, so to fill that void in my life, a mutual acquaintance introduced me to Ghisola, and I started volunteering to help her clean her pens and tend to her dogs. Her family owns saddleback beagles and a line of really nice Llewellin setters. We went on a few bird-and-rabbit hunts together, and after a while, we became regular friends. Eventually we became exceptional friends.

Ghisola and I never had sex, but we certainly did joke about it a lot. A trustworthy companion is a precious thing, but finding just another roll in the hay is as easy as falling off a log, so we certainly didn't want to taint a rare thing for the sake of a common one. Besides, she's a hair-pie-eating tomboy if ever there was one, so she might not have been interested in an actual romance with someone of my demographic.

That's who the police officer was on the night of the robbery. Ghisola didn't know that I knew of Riner Salse's intention to break into the store, and out of concern for her conscience and our friendship, I'll never tell her. This is a deception I need to bear alone. I was learning new ways of doing the right thing in those days, and duplicity and beguilement were among them.

Across the highway from the store Salse planned to rob is a restaurant. I invited Ghisola to pal around a little that Saturday night, intending to take her to the restaurant so she could witness the robbery. I made the plans far in advance so her schedule would be open. I offered to pay, so I knew she would accept. There weren't many options for cooked groceries in that area back in those days, so it's not like I had any trouble making sure we would go to the right place. I just drove there like it was the automatic thing to do.

The town, by the way, is called Malbowges because it sits in the middle of ten canals that drain swamps into Lake Pontchartrain during heavy rains and hurricanes. The burger joint is called Bowges because that's what all the locals call the town.

While I'm in the mood to be handing out proper names, I should say that the store Salse was going to rob is called Sins of the Wolf. To be really specific, only the bar portion of the establishment is called that. The rest is called Wolf's. It's owned by a family named Wolf.

Ghisola and I went to Bowges on the night of the scheduled robbery, and I picked a seat near the window so I could look across the highway at Wolf's. Lo and behold, I saw what looked like trouble across the street. A carload of guys had pulled into the parking lot, and when they tried to get into the store, the door was locked. I joked to Ghisola that Wolf had decided to close up shop early for the first time in history. Then I just sort of breathed the words "That's funny." My plan worked, and Ghisola sauntered over to Wolf's to have herself a look. I expected to hear gunfire any second. It didn't go that way.

A few minutes later, Ghisola came back across the street and into the restaurant and told me that Wolf's car was still parked out back but no one answered the door. I told her it was probably nothing, but if she wanted verification, she should go into the building and check things over. Because she was a female in a gender-nontraditional career, Ghisola was extra cautious about doing anything that looked like it could cause her feelings to override her judgment. I knew about her caution, and I used it to encourage her to not call any more cops. We needed to be alone on this deal.

I told her again there was probably nothing wrong at the store, and I added that if it helped, I could watch the back of the building while she entered through the side. I reassured her that I wouldn't intervene if anything happened and would just yell if I saw anything. Based upon those conditions, she let me participate.

Ghisola gave me a minute to get to the back of Wolf's, and then she entered the door on the side of the building. The Wolf family had been in business for a long time, and they probably knew just about every delivery driver in the area, so the side door didn't get locked much back in those days. It was a nuisance to keep unlocking doors for deliveries, so it was common for small business owners to have an enclosed porch or storage area that remained unlocked.

After a minute, I knew Ghisola would be in the store, so I worked my way close to the back of the building. It took longer than I thought because my toes wanted to grow roots with each step. Luckily, Ghisola is fleet-footed. Salse had already said he'd die before he'd go back to prison, so the main part of my plan was for Ghisola to go into Wolf's, interrupt his crime, and then kill him as he resisted arrest.

I hid myself in a place where I thought I could be inconspicuous, just in case Salse decided to slip out the back as Ghisola entered through the side. That's exactly what happened.

Salse tried to sneak out when he heard Ghisola, and I tackled him from behind. I shoved him back into the building through the half-open exterior door while he was trying to close it silently. It was easy for me to do because he was moving in slow motion. I suppose he was concentrating on not making a sound. I never saw a man look so bug-eye amazed! The poor bastard hardly reacted. I had adrenaline; he had bewilderment.

Salse and I fell through the doorway and grappled in an outer room. He didn't have his gun in his hand, so I had to feel for it in his coat pockets. I found it and yanked it out.

In moments of panic, time crawls. I had such an experience when I was with Salse. It was as though I had all the time in the world. I murmured to him that he was a gone son of a bitch who would wish he were dead after the cops threw him back in jail, and the look on his face transformed from confusion to one of vacuous abandon. As Salse and I were scrambling, I heard Ghisloa's approaching footsteps. I intentionally tossed his gun onto the floor across the room because I wanted him to scramble for it. When Ghisola stepped through the doorway into the outer room with us, all she saw was me diving away and Salse scampering for his pistol. I heard her yell *"Freeze!"* and I heard the shots: *Pop! Pop! Pop!*

In contrast to my clumsiness, Ghisola was as smooth and cool as a raptor. Salse bled and moaned and wiggled for a few seconds, and then he died.

Ghisola really was a hero, because there were a hell of a lot of holes in my plan. Her expertise compensated for my recklessness. Salse would have indeed killed us both if Ghisola hadn't killed him first, but he was no match for her.

Those are the details of how I helped my two friends; Bell has one less enemy, and Ghisola has the police recognition she deserves.

I organized the death of Bell's enemy in order to do him a favor. After I did him the favor, he looked at me in an entirely different way.

Something in me had changed again. I had descended across another downward threshold: the boat ride with Obra and Charon, my project with Obra and Geryon, and now this. But I had acted alone this time. I had strategized and orchestrated the entire event on my own, without telling anyone but a Mafia kingpin, and all I had said to him is that I would get it done. I didn't even tell Ghisola, the woman who was right there in the event with me. That was new behavior for me. I was changing—becoming stronger, but degenerating, and becoming more isolated in my thinking.

CHAPTER 16

Sic Pro Optima

Suddenly on my ear hit a sound of wailing lamentation, and I struggled to see from where it came. At that time my teacher said, "Behold, my son, it draws near—the city of Dis, with its grave denizens, mighty and strong."
Dante Alighieri, from *The Divine Comedy*, "Inferno," canto VIII

B ell told me he appreciated what I had done for him. "Let me know if I can return the favor," he said. He was turning away from me as he spoke the words.

"Now's a good time," I said, stopping him in his tracks.

He laughed quietly and looked at me from under those heavy, intense brows of his. He saw that I was serious. For just the flash of an instant, I saw a look of here-we-go-again in his eyes, but to his credit, he contained it. I can only imagine the long lines of people who see Bell as a resource for getting what they want—money or revenge, mostly. But I was different, and after I told him what I wanted, he seemed genuinely appreciative, not only because I wasn't trying to milk him, but also because I gave him a fresh, new scenario.

I told Bell that I was smart and hardworking, but I also told him I was a coward. He looked puzzled when I said that. He's not the type of man who would have that problem, and even if he did have it momentarily, he would never speak it.

"I need toughness lessons."

"Come again?"

"The closest I come to being brave is being longsuffering, and I need your help to do better than that."

"I'm listening," he said thoughtfully.

I told him he had a professional acquaintance who looked like the toughest man alive, and I asked him to ask his acquaintance to give me lessons in courage and braveness. I told him I was persistent, which is the loser's version of being formidable, but I wanted to upgrade my lot in life. Bell let out a full-blown belly laugh at that. He actually jiggled.

"That's the craziest thing I ever heard of, kid, and believe me, I've heard some crazy shit in my life. But since you did me a favor—and because I like you—I'll honor your request. Besides, I like your name. It brings out the Roman Italian in me. And I liked that story when I was in school. More schools should teach the classics."

"As far as I know, I'm not related to the real one," I quipped with a smile. He laughed.

I told Bell I had a couple of criteria. I said the lessons couldn't kill me or leave me with visible scars, and the teacher couldn't break off anything that wouldn't grow back. Bell agreed, smiling with his eyes and shaking his head the whole time.

The guy Bell knew did contract work. His name was Simon, but people called him Pope. I knew of Pope by his reputation, and I had seen him before, but I had never actually met him. I recognized him as being in charge because when he was around, all the other men in the room began to demonstrate levels of ineptitude that showed respect to the presence of a greater being. It was that shift that defined Pope as being the boss, and it is the reason I requested him as my mentor.

Later, when I actually met Pope face-to-face, I greeted him politely but with unwavering eye-to-eye contact. My demeanor was courteous, but my voice was strong and my handshake was solid. It was the right thing to do. There aren't many moments when a guy like me is actually proud of himself, but that was one of them.

As I begin to write about Pope's influence on me, I want to say that there was something about him that deserves a pause. It was something dark. I don't mean he was evil, because in spite of his profession, he was a good man, and that's the truth. If it's possible to be guilty without being guilty, then Pope was that combination.

I guess the best way I can describe this dark thing about Pope is to say it seemed as though something terrible had been put there, deep within him. It was so deep that it became a part of him, and he didn't try to get it out any more. Since it was there with such largesse, and since he was instrumental in my life, I took it seriously. It was ominous and within him, but he was still a good man. In a much weaker way, that description applies to me, which is probably why I could see this thing in Pope. We recognize our reflections in others way more clearly than anything else about them.

I shadowed Pope from time to time for about half a year altogether, and during that term, I had some of the finest meals at his house I've ever eaten in my life. His wife really liked to cook. Since I do too, we cooked a lot together. While we cooked, we talked. Kitchens are better than carpools that way. Truth be told, I learned as much from her as from him.

During our conversations, I poked at Pope's wife with sarcasm, which is my odd way of communicating fondness. That kind of humor usually gets me in trouble a lot, but with Pope and his family, I fit right in.

As is usually the case with people I like, I had a nickname for Pope's wife. I called her Countess. She liked it. Her real name was Matilda, but I just called her Countess. She was a gifted conversationalist, which is on the list of good things I'll always remember fondly about her. She talked a lot but didn't interrogate me. I like that style. It's interactive but not intrusive.

One particular time when Countess and I were in the kitchen, I said to her that men are better at meal preparation than women, and that's why chefs tend to be men while cooks tend to be women. I didn't really believe it, of course, but I rarely passed up an opportunity to give her a little grief. Without missing a beat, she replied that chefs tend to be men because being a chef is a job, and women tend to be cooks because being a cook is a service. Knowing that serving is always a higher calling than working, I thought she was a genius. I hugged her neck. She told me I smelled good.

Come to think of it, there was another time Countess demonstrated her sharp insight. I use it a lot in my thinking about people, especially regarding people I'm judging to kill, so I should write about it. I need to remember to mention this to Pat.

It happened when Countess gave me a cooking tip, and to her that's all she was doing, but I've used that tip as a metaphor for high-quality work ever since. I listened to Countess each time she taught me something, but this one particular moment I remember especially well.

We were about to make grillade and grits for Pope and the kids, and I was admiring the high quality of the pork and beef Countess had bought. Grillade is a kind of stew-like meal made of meat medallions seared in their own gravy and then ladled onto a plate alongside breakfast foods. The aroma is amazing, and if you want to fill your kitchen with people, just start cooking grillade. It's better than a dinner bell.

Traditionalists serve grillade ladled onto grits, but when I'm alone, I like to make grillade with eggs, not grits. My Yankee upbringing occasionally shows itself in my cooking, and grillade is one of those times. I eat it with toasted baguette bread and piles of extra-sharp cheddar cheese. It's a wonder I don't weigh a thousand pounds.

Countess took particular pride in her grillade. We all have a home base of skills, and this kind of meal was hers.

"I buy only from real butchers," she said to me that day in her kitchen as I admired her pork and beef.

"How do you know when a butcher is real?"

"By asking for stew bones," she said. "If the shop doesn't have marrow bones, then you're buying meat that's been processed elsewhere, and the smiley-faced people standing behind the counter are not real butchers. Sometimes a white apron is just a costume."

I never forgot that advice—every act of genuine labor produces a by-product, so people who are the real deal will be able to produce by-products from their work. Stew bones are a real butcher's by-product.

My early life didn't have a by-product, and if I had known what that meant when I was in my twenties, I would have worked in a way that produced one—a way with much more purpose and direction. Countess gave me insight about many things, including myself, which is why I include her so liberally here in this diary.

Countess informed me through metaphor. I know from my days as a teacher that people "receive" information when it's handed to us, but we "know" what we've figured out on our own, so learning is second-rate if the teacher gives information to us too directly.

A little while later, as we were still cooking the grillade that morning at Pope's house, Countess was talking about wives and religion as usual; and also as usual, I was responding politely but not saying much else. She looked at me quietly for a moment or two and then laid her utensils on the counter and put her hand on my forearm.

"T 'boy," she said, "you pra'lem is dat you ha' too much respec' an not enough fait. This what make you so complicate, an' I hope you stren' overcome you weakness someday."

Her words were crisp and kind, and she pronounced each letter with quickness and precision in that beautifully charming way Cajun women sound when they speak English. Her family must be from Lafayette. I'm not sure what that crispness is called in linguistics, but it's absolutely beautiful, so I hope it has a name. It's the sound of a vocal ballerina—tippy and choppy and light.

I was so shocked by the accuracy of Countess Matilda's analysis of me that I didn't even respond. She nailed it. I had too much respect and not enough faith, and I, too, hope that my strength overcomes my weakness someday.

There are entire years of my marriage I don't recall, and yet I can still see Countess giving me that observation as if it happened just a little while ago. Chronos time is in motion whether we use it or not, but Countess took me into kairos time, which can be an inconstant and interesting thing to reflect upon.

After she told me about respect and faith, Countess inauspiciously turned to the counter and continued working. She took her glasses off and bent close to her work so she could see it better, but she kept talking—as usual. I remember the visual clearly. She was slicing cucumbers. She had macerated chickpeas the day before in a mortar-and-pestle marinade of zesty Italian dressing with a splash of gin and the tiniest drop of hot sauce. She was going to serve the macerated chickpeas on the cucumber slices, using them like crackers. She rubbed the cucumbers in coarse-ground black pepper and added a kind of round-tasting, green-leafy garnish. Kale, she called it. I had never heard of it before that day. Countess was a trendsetter.

I cooked with Countess quite a lot that week. I don't remember why. I guess Pope stayed at home a lot for some reason, and since I was shadowing him, I was there too.

A few evenings later, I was cooking ravioli with Countess, and Pope's children said they preferred my cooking to their mother's. They didn't really mean it, of course. They were just complimenting me as an opportunity to tease her. To get revenge for Countess, I served them one raviolo at a time on a demitasse plate and told them it was all they were going to get because it was all they deserved. I made them beg for more ravioli, but I gave them only one raviolo at a time. Pope laughed raucously.

One of the reasons children tend to love me so readily is that I'm mean to them. Immature palates can't be trusted.

I'm documenting this event now because one of Countess Matilda's occasional topics about their children was very important. She and Pope had a son as their first-born child, and he died a tragic death. It affected Pope deeply, and it paralleled me not more than a year later, so Pat has encouraged me to include it here in my writing.

The death of the boy was heavy, and it explained a lot to me about Pope and his dark side. My similar experience only a year or so later had the exact same effect on me. Fate forced me to follow Pope's example as his protégé into that specific darkness, even to the point of unintentionally mirroring his tragic event.

I didn't ever push Countess for details about their dead son; I just let her bring it up occasionally. I've learned that the best way to get at an important topic is through spontaneous waves of casual conversations delivered in relaxed moments. Human beings aren't capable of communicating complicated topics all at once, so we do it better in thin layers. That's the way Countess communicated about her dead son.

My writing about Pope gives the impression that he grew up in the heart of an urban city, but that's not the truth. When they were young, Pope and his new bride lived in a trailer by a river on the outskirts of West Monroe, of all places.

"We stretched a phone line across the river right after we were married," Pope and Countess told me once, "but we lost it in a storm. A floating stump probably took it. We thought God was punishing us for being uppity, so we didn't try to put another line back. Not long later, we moved our trailer to the highway side of the river. It seemed more Christian."

In spite of all his acquired big-city knowledge, Pope retained those country values within his spirit. I share that kind of contradiction between my viewable persona and what I really am, so that's why I could see the contrast in him. Unlike me, however, Pope seemed to be at peace, so he was not troubled by the conflict between his values and his activities. I, by comparison, was in constant inner torment, and it was getting worse even then.

Over time, Countess told me the details about their son's death. The story is that they moved to New Orleans, and when Pope first started to make some real money, he bought a membership at an elite duck camp in the swamps east of the city. The club is in Maremma's Marsh. It's very private and exclusive in a "sportsman's paradise" kind of way.

Countess told me the men at the camp had a few policies for each other, and for all their easygoing ways, they wanted these policies to be obeyed. Not only would they revoke the membership of any member who violated the rules, but they would also pursue legal action for breach of contract. One particular rule was that no children were allowed on the premises except for social functions at the clubhouse. During those events, members could bring their families to meet each other, but absolutely not other than that. This rule was designed to conceal their hush-hush activities at the clubhouse as well as for the sake of safety among the children. It was a logical idea given the hostile nature of Maremma's Marsh surrounding the camp.

This policy regarding young children is important to remember because Pope broke it regularly by taking his toddler son into the marsh with him. Matilda said his primary motivation for buying the membership in the first place was to spend outdoor time with the boy, so how could Pope resist? She said Pope instructed the child to hide if he ever heard or saw anyone while they were in the marsh. She told me they even went so far as to practice hide-and-seek just to emphasize the need for secrecy with the child.

The short version of the tragedy is that Pope accidentally locked himself in a coffin-style duck blind. The blinds are called that because they look like a coffin and they're designed to be buried at a feet-down angle just below the soil level. Hunters lie in them and close part of a lid while hunting so that waterfowl can't see them, and after the hunt is over, hunters close and lock the entire lid to secure their equipment and keep swamp critters out of the box.

Crawling in and out of the box naturally deposits a little swamp debris, which filters down into the foot area, and because of the design of the box, the only way to clear that debris is to crawl down headfirst and grab it by the handful. Once, while Pope was cleaning the box in that way, he bumped the lid and it closed on top of him. If there had been another adult with him, as was acceptable practice within the club, the adult would easily have been able to unhook the lid and let Pope out, but since no children were allowed on the hunting lease, Pope hadn't told anyone he was there with his son, so they were alone. The child couldn't unhook the lid.

Matilda told me that while the child was trying to let his father out of the box, he heard what he mistakenly thought were the voices of other hunters, so he ran and hid, as he had always been trained to do. She said the child was probably confused because his father wouldn't come out of the box, and Pope told her that he was screaming, which no doubt made the boy hide even more because he could hear the desperation in his father's voice.

For years I have wondered how Pope must have felt during those minutes as he lay at an upside-down angle with his head in the bottom of that coffin blind. He must have felt an enormous relief when he once again heard his son's tiny voice speaking to him from the other side of the lid. I can only imagine how Pope breathed a colossal sigh just before he made a terrible mistake and ended it all.

Pope told Matilda that after repeatedly trying to tell his son how to unlock the doors, he finally gave up in a fit of exasperation. He said being upside-down with his head in the bottom of that coffin blind was making him light-headed, and he was afraid that he and his son would be stranded in the sloughs after dark, where his son would be in peril from the night creatures.

I've been to Maremma's Marsh. The bayou at night is a much less friendly place than during the day. It is not scenic and beautiful during those times. At night, Death is close in Maremma's Marsh, with breath slow, wet, and hungry. I know this from personal experience.

Pope told Matilda he was terrified by knowing he would be able to hear danger verge upon his son and yet be unable to do anything about it. He devised a plan.

Matilda told me that Pope decided to send his son back to the clubhouse while there was still plenty of daylight remaining. He told the boy he should get into daddy's pickup truck and press on the horn until someone came. He told his son not to hide from anyone. He told him to not play or daydream but to go straight to the truck and press the horn. He barked at his son to not do anything but that.

"Come out, Daddy," the child repeated. Matilda said these words haunted Pope horribly, even all those years later.

"*Do as I told you!*" Pope screamed at the boy. Countess said these last words were sharp and stern every time Pope reenacted them, communicating all the anger and frustration he was feeling from within that coffin blind.

Countess said that only moments after Pope heard his toddler son leave, he regretted telling the child to go. He listened for the sound of the horn telling him his son was in the truck, but the sound did not ever come.

After his young son disappeared, Pope spent three days in his crypt. I call it that because some part of him really did die and remain buried there. He emerged a revenant. Changed.

The first night Pope was missing, Matilda said she thought it was odd he didn't call her, but rationalizing that he would have to drive to a payphone to call her, she dismissed her concerns; however, the second night he stayed gone without communication, she grew more alarmed. There were no cell phones in those days; otherwise, she would have simply called him. She was worried, mostly because he had the child with him. Her mind raced. Should she risk expulsion from the club and a possible lawsuit by telling the other members that Pope was there with his son? Ultimately, the other members of the hunting club noticed that Pope's truck had remain unmoved for three days, so they set about looking for him. They found him in the coffin.

Matilda said the coroner could only speculate about what caused the child's death from what was left of his little body. The autopsy report stated simply "Exposure." Countess emphasized that Pope's final words to his son tormented him every day: *Do as I told you!*"

Hell had found Pope, and he decided to share it with the world after that. I know this not because he told me, but because I can absolutely relate. From my own personal experience a year or so later, I know that Pope was cursed to carry that rage within himself for the rest of his life. It explained a lot about him. It explains a lot about me too.

By the time I shadowed him, Pope's general job with the mafia was to arbitrate disagreements between people, and he was in popular demand because he did it well. I think the secret of his success was the abutment of his genuinely nice personality wrapped in a body that could kill you if you didn't comply with his expectations.

It's a common misconception that the Cosa Nostra likes to kill people, for they really don't. They're certainly willing to kill their enemies and detractors, but it's a necessity, not a preference. They're businesspeople, not lunatics.

Occasionally, however, people who opposed his clients would be prideful and inflexible, and Pope would have to brandish his authority. He was so well known in his work that, when he showed up, people usually got correct with each other without Pope having to take any real action. He was better than a priest that way.

Unfortunately, not all people are among the faithful.

CHAPTER 17

Sedition at Camp Hazeroth

I see new sufferings and new sufferers far and wide wherever I move or turn myself to strain my curious eyes. This Fortune, what is it, which has the goods of the world so in its clutches?
—Dante Alighieri, from *The Divine Comedy*, "Inferno," canto VII

On what I think was our most memorable workday together, Pope had been sent to Hammond, a town just to the northwest of New Orleans. It was to be a serious day, and I was fortunate to be allowed to tag along. It was a Saturday. There was a politician in the town who had been put into office by the power brokers in New Orleans in exchange for her loyalty. Her lenders remembered the debt, but she forgot.

This woman had big plans and a fugue-state memory. This is always a poisonous combination. It is detrimental for everyone involved—particularly the amnesiac.

Pope and I drove to Hammond to see the woman. He was partly negotiating with her and partly delivering a message to her and her neighbors in Tangipahoa Parish.

The woman we went to see in Hammond was named Gomita Marchese. I'll never forget that name. I'll also never forget her hairstyle. At a single glance it told of her insecurity as well as her presumption that all expectations must be met without pause. We took her to dinner, and we never took her back. It was my first experience with killing for profit.

I can't quite say I was a hitman just yet, for as usual, I didn't do the actual killing, but neither did I do anything to stop what happened. I had already orchestrated two murders, but those were different. I was implementing justice with those two events. A death is a death is a death, but Gomita's murder was a deeper, darker deed, for this death was for profit, not for amends. That made it feel worse to me, but I still participated. Little by little, we learn to live with the things that bother us, which is what allows moral decay to be a journey downward one step at a time.

A little south of Hammond is a plant that makes telephone poles. It's an interesting place to see from Interstate 12 because all the pine trees being processed there are stacked in a gigantic circle. The limbs are cut off the pines so there's nothing left but the straight trunk. They are stacked with a crane situated in the middle to maneuver the poles from that location.

Specifically, the circle is actually more like a letter *C* because there's a gap where the workers can have an opening to enter and access the equipment. In the center of this area with the crane are all the other pieces of equipment used for turning pine trees into telephone poles. Mostly, the trees are sprayed with a chemical called Bulicame. It's an oily liquid derived from coal tar, and it's used to preserve and disinfect wood. If you touch a telephone pole, especially a new one, Bulicame is the gunk that sticks to your hand—which isn't a bad thing, because Bulicame is also an antiseptic. If it wasn't so nasty, it could probably be prescribed by doctors as a cure-all topical ointment.

When Bulicame gets cold, it gets thick, like tar. In that condition, it's difficult to spray onto the poles, so it has to be kept hot in order to retain its semiliquid state. It's stored in a heating vat at the base of the crane in the center of the *C*. Even when the plant is closed for the weekend, like the Saturday when we were there, the Bulicame is kept at an elevated temperature in the vat so it can be quickly reheated to its workable constitution at the start of the work week.

There are three arms on the crane at the Bulicame plant in Hammond. One arm, the main one, is much larger than the other two because it positions and rotates the layers of poles so they can be repeatedly sprayed with ongoing applications of Bulicame. Another arm, equally long but much less thick, extends a hose and a nozzle that applies hot Bulicame onto the poles. The third arm, much shorter than the first two, is used for lifting fifty-five-gallon drums of cold Bulicame and holding them upside-down while they empty into the heating vat.

This is the place where Pope and I took Gomita Marchese to have a conversation the day we drove to Hammond. Being tucked in the middle of the C-shaped arrangement of poles on a Saturday when no workers were present, I felt ominously secluded, and the heat and odor coming from the hot Bulicame tanks gave the place an even more sinister drift of multisensory severity. I'm pretty sure Pope had this last part in mind all along. The mise en scène punctuated his message.

As we entered the plant and walked into the center of the C-shaped pile of poles, I expected Ms. Marchese to worry about her safety, or at least question our being there, but she didn't. I, on the other hand, don't like nebulous places, so I was feeling a little edgy.

I suspect Ms. Marchese and Pope and their associates had met there before. The meetings must have been frequent enough and varied enough and common enough that Gomita didn't question being taken there. She might have even thought I was the one in danger.

The other thing I thought to be peculiar is that Gomita didn't ask who I was or why I was with them. In fact, she didn't seem to take much stock of me at all. I don't think she was intentionally not seeing me the way Pope's other associates tended to ignore me; I think she was just too damn self-centered to notice that I was actually there. Nothing more than that—just too damn self-centered.

While overhearing their conversation, I was starting to understand not only the purpose of our visit but also its rigor. I already knew

Gomita had made her associates in New Orleans angry when she started a side business selling the justice and power of her public office, but I underestimated the urgency with which they wanted the situation handled. They meant business.

Organized crime in New Orleans doesn't have anything against illegality in general, but it tends to resent being cut out of the profits—particularly when they're the ones who situated the profiteer in the first place. Earlier that day, as we arrived to meet Gomita, Pope gave me what few details I needed to have to understand the day's purpose. He also gave me his usual stay-quiet-and-out-of-the-way speech. I complied. I was Gomita's opposite.

During the meeting, the three of us—Pope, Gomita Marchese, and I—stood on a deck attached to the cranes in the center of the circle of poles. Altogether, the deck was fifteen or twenty feet above the ground and designed to provide access to the open vat of hot Bulicame beneath it. It was probably eight or ten feet above the surface of the molten sludge, which was itself something like eight or ten feet deep.

Pope and Gomita were talking. Actually, he was talking but she was telling. There's a difference. She was so focused on her demands that she didn't even notice when Pope led her out onto a metal grate above that open vat of steaming goo, and yet, lo and behold, there we were.

There was no one there but the three of us on the platform that Saturday. The C-shaped pile of poles was about three stories high, and its outer edges were about as big in diameter as half a football field. Even though the facility is within easy sight of Interstate 12, a grenade could have gone off inside that circle with us, yet nobody on the outside would have known.

Pope's message was simple. He was telling Gomita that she should share her sideline profits as a gesture of goodwill if nothing else.

"After all," he said, "they're the ones who made you what you are. You wouldn't be able to earn this extra money if it weren't for them."

"Look," she said, "I already send the agreed-upon chunk of my earnings back to those bastards in New Orleans, so if I can harvest an additional gain for myself, why is that any of their business? Let's get something straight; they got me elected with the understanding that I would do two things: always vote as they told me to vote, and send them a percentage of the construction projects they swung in my direction. I've always upheld my end of that bargain without compromise or delay, but anything more I earn should be my business alone."

In a legitimate line of work, Gomita would have had a strong case, but in the bed she made for herself, she was without a prayer. Illicit partnerships have their disadvantages, and one of those disadvantages is that rules tend to change as the game goes on. As any trophy fish hanging on a wall will symbolize, sometimes a tasty opportunity comes wrapped around a hook.

Gomita told Pope she knew things that could get people in trouble and she was prepared to use that knowledge. She seemed to be losing her temper increasingly with each word.

The next thing I knew, Pope hit Gomita with his fist. Then he hit her again. Then again. And again. Every time he did it, the smell of Bulicame grew more pungent in my nostrils. I never noticed before that day how blood and Bulicame smell alike, but since then, I can't walk past a new telephone pole without seeing Gomita Marchese's battered face or imagining the taste of cast-off blood in my mouth.

Eventually Gomita landed in a heap on the metal grate. She didn't fall lengthwise; she collapsed straight down onto the top of her shoes, just like the way Cass dropped onto the pavement after Brute hit her. I guess that's how people fall when they're crazy enough to stay in a fight long past time to quit, and even though they're as tough as nails, there's nothing left to hold them up after their strength of will has been beaten out of them. Sane people like me capitulate too quickly to experience anything like that. Once we realize we're not going to win the hot dog–eating contest, we figure we might as well not make ourselves sick by staying in the challenge.

Gomita made quite a clatter as she hit the metal deck, yet the loudest noise of all came from her wedding ring as it smacked against the grate with an indignant *Ping!* It's fascinating how, of all that was going on right then, one noise made by a tiny band of gold would be the most memorable thing for me. *Pinggggg!*

Off to one side of the raised metal deck where we stood is a pipe railing with a control panel mounted on the topmost pipe. The controls operated the three hydraulic arms, including the small one that dumped new barrels of Bulicame into the heating tank below us. The control panel also operated a series of automated hooks and chains attached to the outermost tip of the arm. Pope grabbed an automated hook and attached it to one of Gomita's ankles as she lay on the floor of the grate. The hook had to be operated remotely from the control panel, so attaching it took some skill. Pope seemed to know exactly how the gizmo operated, I noticed.

Skillfully using the control panel, Pope hoisted Gomita by that one leg. She started to curse and flail. I guess I expected a cri de coeur, but she sounded more angry than fearful.

Gomita was wearing a business dress. I don't remember the color, but I do remember that the skirt was mostly hanging around her neck as she dangled upside-down. Pope swung the arm of the pulley out over the pit below, and Gomita started to curse louder as she looked down and saw the brackish surface of Bulicame beneath her.

While I watched, Pope walked down the steps of the platform and fully lit the main heaters on the Bulicame container. The gas burners took fire with a whoosh, and the smell of half-burned, newly lit combustibles filled my nostrils.

I was thinking that Pope sure did seem to know a lot about how this equipment operated, but, like I said before, I think he and Gomita had been there already—probably regularly. There are a lot of treatment plants like this, and Pope might have worked at one in his earlier life. He might have even worked at this very plant. It's a bad idea to impose the limits of our knowledge on others—especially others like Pope.

Gomita was tethered to her pain for the dozen minutes it took the vat of Bulicame beneath her to percolate. It wasn't quite liquefied by then, but it was certainly thin enough for a human to sink to the bottom.

Pope calmly and quietly walked back up the metal stairs of the platform and stood at the edge of the railing beside me while he waited for the bubbling to accelerate. He unexcitedly lit a cigarette and looked around a couple of times to confirm that we were still alone. Other than that, he just watched Gomita squirm over the heating brew.

When the liquid had barely started to simmer, Pope reached over to the control box and swung the hydraulic arm back toward the rail where we were standing. Gomita dangled on the end of the chain like a meat pendulum and plunked against the metal pipes that formed the railing. Some bony part of her body must have hit the metal, because it made a *kung* sort of noise. In spite of what must have been terrible pain, she had the presence of mind to grab the railing before she could bounce away from it. She held herself there, and Pope walked to her and knelt beside her face to talk.

For a second—only a second—I thought Pope was going to reprimand her and then let her off the hook. Literally.

At that moment, Gomita did an incredibly stupid thing. She let go of the railing and spun herself around so she could use her free leg to try to kick Pope as she was swinging back out over the open vat of Bulicame. As rope-a-dope strategies go, hers was flawed. After all, she was, in literal fact, hanging by one leg upside down over a bubbling brew of death. The hem of her skirt tapped her neck, and her pantyhosed crotch was in full view of the open sky while her cotton-clad ass shined bright in the sun for the entire world to see, and she decided this was the perfect time to lash out at her captor. Darwin would have had a field day studying her.

When Gomita tried to kick him, Pope easily leaned off to the side an inch or so, and she missed him entirely. Her shin bashed against the pipe railing. It made almost the same sound I heard when she bounced against the railing a few moments earlier, except that this time it had a kind of creepy resonance that lumbered up and back the full length of the pipes. The first time I heard that *kung* sound, Gomita grabbed the railing and held herself against it, but this time her shin just banged against it like a baseball bat and bounced off again, so there was nothing to deaden the residual pulsation. Even as that haunting sound lingered in my ears, the jerk of her body yanked the chain through the skin of her Achilles heel, and blood ran over her upside-down shin past her knee and onto her thigh. Creepy resonance notwithstanding, that kick was a seriously bad idea.

I think Gomita blanked out after she tried to kick Pope. She had spit up a little vomit, and mucus was running across her face and dripping off her hair. When it landed on the percolating Bulicame beneath her, it didn't even make a ripple. It just plopped onto the goo and stayed there momentarily like a splat of bird shit, and then a bubble ate it.

As I looked at Gomita, I knew her to be one of the toughest people I had ever seen in my life. I think it's true that we learn from fools and from sages alike, because right then I learned something from Gomita Marchese—I saw what toughness was. Toughness is the ability to take a punch without changing our minds. The trouble is, the people who have that skill seem to take it too far. Gomita is a good example of that. Her toughness was her weakness.

When Gomita tried to kick him, Pope quit talking. He stood fully beside her and looked down at her mucus-covered face. He was expressionless. He looked as though he was remembering something from long ago. Soon he seemed to get over it, and he made the barely perceptible gesture of a shrug. He slapped Gomita's upturned fanny, moved the hydraulic arm out over the center of the percolating Bulicame vat, and flicked a switch that released the electric hook from her ankle. She dropped instantaneously.

In my mind's eye, I watched Gomita Marchese fall for about ten seconds down into the scorching vat beneath her. She hit like a calving iceberg.

After Gomita fell into the pit below, Pope and I watched quietly for a few moments. He was standing off to my side on the deck. He was close to the railing, but unlike me, he wasn't leaning against it for support. We were looking down at a sharp angle, standing motionless, our necks bent and our hands in the pockets of our overcoats, perfectly still like a couple of well-dressed gargoyles, watching the Bulicame settle into a state of quiet rest.

After but a short while, the boiling vat of Bulicame looked as if it had never been disturbed. Pope walked across the deck to turn off the hydraulic machinery and then returned to stand by my side. Without moving my body, I slowly turned my face toward Pope. He was quietly looking down again to where he had plunged Gomita to her death. I had the feeling the two of them went back a long way. He looked at the place where she vanished as if it were a mile beneath him.

Standing there on that grate as we watched all evidence of Gomita disappear, I did the only bold thing I have ever done with Pope. I asked him an uninvited, personal question.

"Mark," he answered after a while, slowly and clearly, "you should never try to deceive and impress the same people." He did not look at me while he spoke but instead kept his face pointed at the Bulicame.

Pope turned and adjusted several things on the deck, and he then walked down the stairs to turn off the burners and finish with the machinery at ground level. When he was done, he looked up at me standing on the platform and calmly said, "It's time to go, Mark." His tone was softer and more paternal to me than it had ever been before. He didn't tell me what to do; he just described the situation like a loving parent speaking to a well-behaved child.

I turned and walked slowly across the platform to the top of the steps. With the machinery now off, I could hear to the swish of traffic on the interstate not far away. My state of mind sat heavily upon me, for I was fully realizing that I had deliberately abandoned faith in all my foundational values. I was capable of being in the presence of extraordinarily brutal events without imposing any judgment upon them whatsoever. I had certainly changed.

Our mood was solemn while Pope and I took leave of that hollow. As I walked down the metal steps to him from the platform, I heard a curious thing. Way off in the distance, I heard the soft, hollow sound of my own footsteps dropping lower and lower. It wasn't an echo; it was the actual sound of my feet on the metal steps beneath me. But more than that, it was the emblematic resonance of my own moral decay speaking directly to me. Imprecation is a powerful thing.

CHAPTER 18

Bathsheba's First Baby

Then was the point upon which all weight bears down from everywhere. Ask me not for details, Reader, for I shall not waste time writing what words are powerless to express.
—**Dante Alighieri, from *The Divine Comedy*, "Inferno," canto X**

I could still have turned back to my law-abiding lifestyle around that time, because not long after Gomita's death, I met a woman and was genuinely falling in love. Besides, darkened as I was, I had yet to actually kill anyone. I had been present at the murders of three people, and I had orchestrated two of those murders, but I had not yet directly done any killing. Soon after that, two things happened: first, I did something beyond which a man can never recuperate, and second, Obra died. Those two things hit me at a pivotal point in my recuperation, and my lot was sealed into rampage.

I was thirty-five years old that year, and even beyond my singular misfortune, the calendar was off to a terrible start: Bill Clinton had recently become president, Islamic fundamentalists bombed the World Trade Center, and the Waco siege ended in a deadly fire. One might expect that my alcoholic tendencies would flare uncontrollably during all that gloom, but ironically, I didn't touch a drop. The only good news that year was Beanie Babies.

A half dozen years after that, in the late 1990s, a movie came out called *The Matrix*. It was a great movie in many ways, but one particular scene encapsulated my transition so precisely that it sticks with me even now. As I write these words, a decade has passed since that movie opened, so I'll have to paraphrase the details, but the essence is that Laurence Fishburne's character was mentoring Keanu Reeves's character about life choices. He used a metaphor of pills: select a blue pill and live a subjugated life of ignorance and bliss, or select a red pill and live an unshackled life of awareness and hardship. Before my unforgivable sin and Obra's death, I would gladly have taken the blue pill of clueless satisfaction.

I was around four decades old when I watched *The Matrix*, and since I had already lived an extraordinary life by then, I brought no small amount of hard-knocks perspective into that scene. In fact, I had enough perspective to see the flaw of the meme, and that flaw is this: not everyone is given a choice between pills.

Early in my life, I would have taken the blue pill so fast that I wouldn't even have heard about the red-pill option, but Moirai took a hand and shoved the red pill down my throat. As I said, not everyone is given a choice between pills. It really is possible to be born under a dark cloud with only red-pill options.

As any student of theater will attest, none of the players on stage can change the fate of their characters. We can add a personal touch, such as how we move and how we say our lines, but we cannot change the role we play. Fate will have her way. That's that.

In the life of every tragic character, there's always an inciting incident leading to a point of no return. Beyond that, the protagonists must acknowledge that their lives have taken a no-going-back change of direction, and they have no choice but to embrace their newfound, irrevocable, unchosen, predestined causatum.

Kevin Bruce and Pat have been a godsend by trying to help me move beyond my tragedies and achieve my denouement, but even their tremendously restorative powers have limits. Now, after all this time, I still do better on some days than on others.

The story of the woman I loved is this: my relationship history is full of women who led me out onto the ledge of sanity and abandoned me stranded there, but 1993 was different because she reversed the trend. She's the only woman who ever bothered to talk me off the ledge and bring me back inside to the comfort and safety of the room. She's Mediterranean by heritage, specifically Greek-Italian. Maybe that has something to do with it. Classical literature is full of Latin-Roman heroines who share her abilities.

I loved her very much. I asked her to marry me once, but she said she needed time to work things out within her family first. She didn't straight-out reject my proposal, but I still suffered a bruised ego because she dang sure didn't say yes!

Months later, she told me the likelihood of my success had improved and that I should ask her again. I was in the process of planning that second proposal when I did what I did and blew my chances with her forever. I'm pretty sure her family still wants to kill me and always will. I don't blame them.

The woman I loved had a baby. He was not quite old enough to be a toddler, and I had grown to love him as my own. I love them still, especially the baby, which is why out of genuine affection for them I cannot write their names here in this tainted account.

My terminus happened in mid-July of 1993. The weather was very, very hot that year, even by Louisiana standards. We'd had a good celebration a couple of weeks prior to that on the Fourth with the woman's family. I remember from the party that the baby was learning to walk but couldn't quite yet do it. Her family is large, so there were a lot of people with us at the picnic. It was a good chance for me to showcase my equipment and skills from the barbecue businesses. I was happy.

Independence Day isn't a traditional holiday among immigrants, but I brought a lot of Anglo into the mix. Besides, with my alfresco cooking skills, what Mediterranean matriarch could refuse a midsummer gathering? Even under that oppressive heat, we had a great time. I loved the family as if I belonged biologically. They gave me a feeling of home.

The exact date of my offence was July 27, 1993. I'll never forget that date, because in addition to my own personal tsunami, the Italian mafia bombed Vatican City. For patriotic and cultural reasons, the family was terribly upset; and for theological reasons, so was I.

When it happened, I was driving my car with the baby behind me in his car seat. I was listening to the news on the radio about the bombing, remembering the Fourth of July celebration, and organizing the new marriage proposal in my mind. Since I had so much happening mentally, I didn't notice Obra's car in the oncoming lane until we were nearly past each other. I glanced quickly into the rearview mirror to try to see if he had seen us, but I couldn't tell, so I turned my head around and looked directly through the rear window of the car. I only looked back for a second—only a second—and then I glanced down at the baby in his car seat. He was sound asleep. I liked it. I looked back up through the rear window at Obra's car. That's when it happened.

I imagine Obra was doing the same thing as me when he hit the car head-on. He probably looked over his shoulder for a second, but in that second, he swerved into the oncoming lane. I saw the whole thing.

I screeched to a stop, parked my car on the side of the highway, jumped out, and sprinted the quarter mile or so back to him. I don't know why I didn't just drive back to the scene of the accident. That would have been the sensible thing to do, but who thinks of such things at a time like that? I was pure muscle and impulse. My amygdala was raging.

Obra's skin was waxy white when I first reached his side, probably from a loss of blood. He was in shock. I'll never forget the feel of his body as I cradled him in that puddle of blood amid the bystander's panicky clamors of "What should we do? What should we do?"

"Get to a phone and call 911," I heard myself shouting. I don't know how many times I said it. Probably a lot. That part is a blur. Obra was bleeding terribly, and I was trying to stop it.

"What should we do? What should we do?"

"Call 911!"

"What should we do? What should we do?"

"Call 911!"

People were screeching their words and starting to panic. We all have our emotional hot buttons, and one of mine is impatience with people who are capable of only the fun and happy events life has to offer, particularly if they use someone else's tragedy to overdramatically seek sympathy for themselves. They make me lose my mind a little. The group of bystanders wobbled while the heroic ones comforted the traumatized ones. As I thought of Obra suffering and losing blood, I made myself stop wasting time on the losers at the scene. With determined intentionality, I put my mind exclusively and forcefully on Obra.

I'm not sure how long that part went on, but I realized no ambulance in the world could get there in time to save Obra considering his rate of blood loss, so I picked him up and carried him to a nearby delivery van. The driver saw me coming and opened the door. I chucked Obra into the back of the van and jumped in with him. The driver hit the gas even as I was shutting the door.

"If you see emergency lights coming, flag them down and we'll transfer him," I said.

"I'll do it!" the driver shouted over her shoulder to me while I was in the back of the van with all the packages, struggling to stop Obra's bleeding. Her competence comforted me.

We passed no emergency vehicles on the road. By the time we arrived at Ochsner, Obra was dead in my arms. We didn't carry cell phones in those days. I was hoping one of the panicky people back at the scene of the accident had left the spectacle and gone somewhere to find a phone to dial 911. But when I checked with EMS, it turned out nobody had. These thoughts have fueled my warpath against all humanity ever since that day.

I forgot about the baby in the car. He died of heatstroke while I was in the emergency room at Ochsner with Obra. I thought of him while I was there, but it was already too late.

The emergency room staff called the police immediately, but when they reached him, he was dead. Now Pope and I have something horrible in common, and I completely understand him. These days when I enter a room, all the other men begin to demonstrate levels of ineptitude that shows respect to the presence of a greater being. It is in their best interest to behave that way, for hell has found me, and I am eager to share it.

CHAPTER 19

Dance Macabre

I shed no tear nor spoke a word, all that day nor the next
night, until another sun rose on the world.
—**Dante Alighieri, from *The Divine Comedy*, "Inferno," canto XXXIII**

One thing led to another, and eventually my real opportunity to kill a lot of people came from the mayor herself. I was one of a team of specialists.

Crime in the Deep South has always been an issue, but the genteel culture has a way of seeing only what it wants to see, so most citizens turn a blind eye to criminality. Unfortunately, the thing we ignore tends to grow. After a while, we still want to ignore it, but it becomes distracting, and we need to make it go away. Eventually the elephant in the room is going to poop, and the crime epidemic grazing across New Orleans was showing signs of hoisting its tail.

The mayor was under increasing pressure from the electorate to do something about lawlessness; however, the citizenry damn sure wouldn't support any nightly news showdowns. The electorate wanted something done, but it didn't want anything to happen.

The blunt version of this story is that the mayor sent out a team of talent scouts who located and hired people to quietly remove the hobgoblins and wastrels from society. One of my regulars during the Zero Risk Bias phase of my businesses worked for the mayor as a talent scout in this capacity. He stood by me at the smoker, visiting, more times than I can remember. I came to know him quite well through these conversations, and, reciprocally, he came to know me.

The guy who recruited me to work for the mayor approached me carefully when he talked about the prospect. Antaeus was his name; he was a giant of a man. He said it would be an honor for me to do the job. He said it required a hard-to-find combination of desirable characteristics. He said I fit the profile perfectly and that I was a rare man in valuable ways.

I had made a lot of money selling my cooking businesses, and more money in the pull phase, so I had the luxury of being able to afford to take a job just because it so perfectly fit my very rare combination of hard-to-find, desirable characteristics. Heck, who can pass up an offer like that? "It's an indispensable honor, Mark, and you're perfect for it." Antaeus left out the part where most of my "perfection" was being a morally bankrupt errand boy haunted by inner demons and disappointed by the failures and disasters of his past.

I was still making money when Antaeus came to see me, but only through investments. The working phase of my life was over. After Katrina hit the South and devastated all the coastal states in 2005, I invested my money wisely and made more. Mountains more. Damn big mountains more. Thinking about those investments tells me what a declined person I had become. I felt that if America had chosen to shun the honorable ideology of my youth in favor of options that are quick, cheap, and easy, then I could surely reciprocate by using that stupidity to put some cold, hard cash in my pocket.

As my moneyed acquaintances and I strategized our investments in the aftermath of Katrina, most of the group talked about generators and water purifiers and hand tools—things like that. It made perfect sense; however, having lost all respect for humanity, I was not of a rebuilding mindset in those days. Not anymore.

In government terminology, New Orleans is officially classified as a "nonregime city," which means there's not a lot of centralized control or overarching authority. This is a genteel way of saying people can't be made to do what they don't want to do, even if they're in charge of getting it done. On ordinary, uneventful days, this is fine, but during periods of disaster response and relief, it's a problem.

After months of delays following Katrina, the federal government and FEMA finally got around to stepping in with actual cash assistance to try to overcome what our dysfunctional local leaders couldn't do, but by then, people had already crawled back up again, so the rescue money went into discretionary purchases, not survival. I've already written that when Obra was alive, he taught me to pay attention to what's not happening more than to what is happening, so seeing a void where rational purchases should have been, I offered irrational alternatives.

Money landed in piles upon people who didn't know what to do with it. What the funding lacked in timeliness it made up for in volume. Unfortunately, blasts of cash usually don't turn into decisions of improvement for witless people. I capitalized on that reality.

Since feel-good moments are rare in feel-bad environments, struggling masses are typically unprepared for the burdens of success. After climbing a hill of hardship, the dale of comfort is a curse of ease, and that's usually the phase of a journey where untried people get into trouble because they don't know ahead of time that they should prepare for downhill residuum. Traveling a dale uses a different set of muscles from climbing a hill, but the traverse is equal in difficulty, and not a lot of people are strong in that way. A dale should be a sojourn, but it's actually where most people find their ruin. History is fat with examples of people who thrive under the burdens of poverty only to be undone by a life of plenty.

Knowing that people in the presence of cash tend to develop short-term thinking, I set up opportunities to buy overpriced experiences that made them happy. I also implemented mandatory interdepartmental supply chains and internal payment transfers, so my own departments were not only my highest-paying customers but were also places that buried the flow of cash. Some of my employees couldn't resist the temptation to steal from me, but I turned a blind eye to it because graft encourages poor bookkeeping practices. They erased their own connection to the money, and by virtue of that behavior, they erased my connection too. My bank accounts were busting, but my spirit knew no joy.

I broke about a zillion laws during those days yet never was chased by the police, let alone caught. There may have been some drug-addled recollections and talk on the streets among my customers about me, but with the police having caseloads already packed, they weren't about to chase the vaporized lore of a "some guy" memory like that. Too bad, for I was genuinely evil.

My friends' hardware investments paid back their principal and earned about a fourth every year on top of that, which is a pretty good percentage; however, by contrast, my sins-of-the-flesh investments hovered around 1,000 percent profit annually—sometimes more.

I provide those details now only to clarify in my brain where my life was at the time Antaeus came to talk to me. It's an understatement to say I was in a financial position to accept the honor of working for the mayor. When Antaeus approached me with cajolery about having the perfect combination of attributes, I leapt at the chance, for it was money I had but purpose I lacked, and Antaeus's offer gave me purpose.

It turns out leaping at flattery was my version of spending windfall money. I am not better than poor folk after all; I'm just spendthrift with a different kind of currency.

We killed people. That was the job. We killed lots of them. I had a little amateur practice with Obra and Geryon, with Ghisola and Salse, and with Pope and Gomita, but that was nothing compared to what I did working for the mayor. After a period of internship and practice, I became good at it—very, very good at it. I was a tortured soul.

I really did kill a boatload of slugs, but I won't write a lot of specifics here in this diary. I'm writing for purpose of calming my dissonance and reestablishing equilibrium, so only the pattern of my mental decay is relevant here in this diary. In spite of the seriousness of the activity, most of the people I killed are not germane to this context. Besides, out of respect to my colleagues, I will not be one to kill and tell. Murder is still illegal, after all.

The mayor's organization was a formal, well-managed operation. This kind of arrangement happens in more cities than you would like to know, and none of us talk about the details. Like all caliphates, this is not a group that will appreciate a showboating commentariat.

The nature of our work was highly volatile and potentially factious, so we had to take interorganizational precautions. That expectation was designed partly for our safety and partly because the mayor really did want this to be a quiet operation, free of press and clamor. We were strongly encouraged to kill people in a way that simply made them go away. The mayor didn't want criminals in her city, but neither did she want a rising homicide rate. She just wanted undesirables to disappear. That's what we made happen. It required finesse, strength, and an ironclad stomach. I was excellent at it because I had all those skills. We could identify and kill anyone we wanted as long as we could justify to our supervisors that our targets were toxic to the holistic public good.

Nobody knew. We had immunity and safety nets to protect us, but we were not unfettered. We had very strict guidelines. We called them "primary directives." For instance, we were prohibited from killing our own enemies if the sole purpose of the hit was vendetta. That is the line that separates soldiers from criminals. In addition to being unprofessional, killing our enemies also had the risk of connecting us to the crime. Suspicion equals attention, and we wanted none of either.

One of our strongest primary directives was that we couldn't demonstrate prejudice. Since we were public employees, we were forbidden from targeting any one type of group. Having a variety of targets was a must, and I supported that philosophy because prejudice is a lazy way of bettering society. We weren't lazy.

Speaking of not being lazy, we were required to design one-off techniques, meaning we couldn't kill two people in the same way. This turned out to be harder than I initially thought, because we all have a go-to bag of tricks, and I certainly have mine. The way I battled repetition was to set up third-person murders, meaning I'd create circumstances in which a seriously bad person would get angry with a moderately bad person to the extent that the moderately bad person would disappear. As long as I could document a trail of cause-and-effect circumstances to my supervisor, I would get credit for the deed.

Perhaps our most important directive was that we were prohibited from harming each other—not even allowed to engage in so much as a practical joke. We couldn't be cross with each other without being asked to take a leave of absence. Ours needed to be a flawlessly loyal group, very difficult to get into, and we were selected for our ability to be steadfast as much as for our abilities to kill and keep quiet. We didn't violate our loyalty directive, and along with my own amnesty, it's one of the main reasons why I offer no specifics here in this diary.

Our work was totally secretive, and we communicated in code. Some of it was standardized, but most of it evolved through familiarity and abbreviated usage. For instance, the organization itself was called "the Club." Members were called "colleagues."

The person we planned to kill was called a "bullseye." Partners added confidential metaphors and inside jokes to that word to make it apply specifically to just one person. This is communication that only longstanding personal experience can translate, thereby making it just about impossible to decipher. The more tomfoolery and tommyrot we included in our gibberish, the harder the argot was to crack. Syllogisms and enthymemes are meaningful because they develop spontaneously among people who have experienced something together, and that's why outsiders cannot crack that kind of code. It's very tight—almost telepathic.

By the way, we never used our real names. When we needed to be specifically identified, the Club used pseudonyms. Even they were obscure.

In point of fact, we had two pseudonyms: one a nickname and the other a codename. The nickname was verbal, and the codename was formal, for paperwork, like performance evaluations and payroll deductions and vacation records.

I'd like to tell you we had pseudonyms like "Thor" or "Lightning" or "Minotaur," but in truth, each nom de guerre was usually humbling. It was part of a corporate strategy to encourage us to not take ourselves too seriously. We used epithets. The nicknames were double-dipped in slur so they were even more insulting than the codenames. For instance, my nickname was "Elbows," acquired because of my tendency to keep my hands in my pockets when I'm not actively busy.

My codename for paperwork was "Mike Stand." It's a play on words for my ability to be unnoticed, like a microphone stand, right there in front of a crowd of people, yet unobserved. I was good that way—nondescript. I brought out the prosopagnosia in all people. A heliotrope is a stone which has magical powers to make its bearer invisible, and jokes throughout the Club suggested I had one in my pockets. I told them that's why I kept my hands there—to protect my heliotrope.

Invisibility may have been useful, but it had an undesirable feature. Who wants to be inherently overlookable? Maybe that's why I punched the guy in the throat for accosting the waitress in the parking lot. I was offended by the way he didn't see me. I'll have to talk to Pat about that.

My knack for invisibility was never clearer to me than one day decades ago when a police officer pulled me over for speeding. A few years earlier, when I was a teacher, he was a student in my class. In ironic fact, he often sped past me while we were driving to school, then he teased me about it later in the classroom in front of his buddies. I recognized him when he was writing the speeding ticket and tried to strike up a conversation, but he drew a blank. I'm not making up this story. It really happened.

"Who was your English teacher?"

"Some guy ..."

He wasn't pretending. The police officer was just that dense, and he didn't remember me. I don't know which made me feel more stultified: not being remembered, or having him blow me off the road, mock me for it in front of my students, and then write me a speeding ticket only a few years later. An event like that cannot be left out of my diary.

Such is my ubiety, and therefore, my ability to intermingle unseen. It was invaluable to me as a colleague in the Club. It helps that I look like an honorable fool—someone easily outsmarted. I inspire other people to feel confidence in themselves, which is important for me to state in exactly that phraseology, because "con" in "con artist" stands for "confidence." That's me—the confidence artist. I'm invisible, comforting, and easily dismissed. I do not inspire fear, worry, or suspicion. Then I kill you. Then I evaporate. So do you.

I loved being in the Club. I was really making a positive difference. It was a hard, ugly job, but it was valuable, and the city was, literally and immediately, a better place for my efforts. It was exactly the career destination I had been wanting all along.

Sadly, it's true that all good things come to an end, and sure enough, the Club eventually began to unravel. Social initiatives are usually successful when they're new. That's the first generation. Unfortunately, success attracts deleterious people. That's the second generation. Second-generation initiatives are usually caustic to the greater good. The first word ever spoken was a wonderful, glorious event for humanity, but the second word spoken was probably a lie. That's just the way we people undo things. Unchecked, a parasite will always kill its host, even though, logically, that's a bad idea.

Some situations are worth fighting for, and some are worth leaving; the hard part is knowing which is which. When he was alive, Obra regularly said we should work to solve our problems but learn to live with our circumstances. But here again, the hard part is knowing which is which. Facts and truth tend to reveal themselves in slow sprinkles over time. As usual, I made plans to leave. The year was 2008.

There's a little town just to the northwest of New Orleans called Madisonville. I made plans to go there to look for real estate. It was a pleasant day, so about midday, I took a break and stopped at a restaurant to have some lunch. The waitress gave me a cup of Community Coffee. It contained chicory. While I was trying to decide how I felt about the chicory, a man accosted my waitress after her shift.

CHAPTER 20

Judas Kiss

Malice forgets both love of kinship and love from Above, so in the
smallest circle down, that dark spot of ice, core of the universe
and throne of Dis, these traitors lie, and they die not.
—Dante Alighieri, from *The Divine Comedy*, "Inferno," canto XXXIV

For all her refined plans, the mayor wasn't immune to betrayal, and she was assassinated in March. The Ides of March. That was a month or so ago. This year is 2010. I am in my early fifties and have had my fill of death. I had no prior knowledge of the mayor's impending assassination, and I had nothing to do with the event. Best now that we bury her and leave it at that.

Maybe it was a group of people who killed the mayor. Reliable rumor has it this was an inside job, and further rumor has it my old pal Cass had her hallmark all over the situation. So did the guy she called Brute. I have known Cass for a decade and a half, and I remember well her need to attain glory by saving the orphanage from the Frankenstein monster. I also remember her willingness to invent a monster if one wasn't available.

The mayor's reputation wasn't winning her any friends in those last days, so apart from grandstanded portrayals, investigations into her demise have been half-hearted at best. Somewhere along the line, she learned she could be a roaring horse's ass to everyone within reach as long as she positioned herself behind a sacrosanct cause, but her strategy eventually failed because even the force field of heroism wears thin after a while.

People who feel impostor syndrome will often replace strength with abuse, and she made many enemies through that mistake. She didn't know what she was doing, and she compounded it by taking advice from the wrong people. Toward the end, she countered her harsh treatment of others by being extra indulgent with herself. Odd how she interpreted those behaviors as balancing her situation. All hell broke loose.

Cass had been on the news quite a lot around that time, proclaiming the mayor's damaged reputation far and wide. She had indeed invented a Frankenstein monster. Una cosa fatta non puo essere disfatta.

In every human collective, there's an in-crowd and an out-crowd. That vogue constantly evolves, and sometimes the crowd of nouveau efficacious people is made up of previous outsiders. In my observation, they are the most abusive leaders of all, and they eventually emblemize the exact behaviors they originally revolted to oppose. As Pat told me when we first started my therapy, we adopt the behaviors of those people who occupy out thoughts, and disruptive activists are mentally obsessed with their enemies, so they become like them. That pendulum was in full swing inside the mayor's head just prior to her murder. She started her career as a public servant, but in the end, she was just another big-bellied fat cat—all five feet and one hundred pounds of her.

My summary of what happened is that the mayor was running for reelection when she and Cass devised a plan to split the opposition by putting in a fake candidate so similar to her opponent that the fake would split that party's votes. The fake candidate was Brute, the guy who punched Cass at the bus stop beside the car showroom.

Brute, as it turns out, doesn't have a legitimate credential on his entire, sad résumé. In spite of that, guys like him can still be useful because their antics are a lot of fun to watch. If I've learned anything in my life, it is that fun-to-watch will always trump legitimacy.

The mayor and Cass encouraged Brute to run for office and ramp up his wacky hijinks to attract a lot of attention. His assignment was to upset the apple cart of public sentiment and associate that negativity with the mayor's opponent so severely that one of two things would happen: he would either steal some votes away from the mayor's opponent, or the general populace would want neither Brute nor the opponent to win the race and would then see Her Honor as a preferable alternative to both of these goofballs. The trouble was that the mayor's thinking was outdated. She didn't realize that hoopla creates success these days, no matter the details, so Brute's campaign, for all its ridiculousness, started to gain traction. Real traction. Noticeable traction. That's when Cass betrayed the mayor and encouraged Brute to seek the office for real. He was a mess. Only sophisticated brains can receive new information gracefully, and this situation was constantly being strafed with changing scenarios. Brute was in over his head.

I was fine with all this because it didn't involve me, but then Cass invited me to her office to discuss Brute's campaign. When I told Pat about the invitation, she very much objected.

"She's a horrible influence on you, Mark! Don't go!"

Kevin Bruce disagreed. He doesn't like Cass, so when he encouraged me to go see her, I was a little surprised. Doubling my surprise was that Kevin Bruce normally agrees with everything Pat has to say. Simultaneously he was encouraging me to see someone he didn't like and disregarding someone he did like. As I have written numerous times already, a break in normal rhythm should be an alarm clock to our sensibilities, because it communicates that something important is up.

In addition to Kevin Bruce's one-eighty, Pat's obdurate admonition for me to not have a meeting with Cass also struck my out-of-rhythm sensibilities. I comprehend the logic behind what she said, but why was she so outspoken about it? Normally she discussed choices with me but didn't give me commands. Was she developing feelings for me? Was she jealous?

Cass said she wanted to see me because I was rich and she needed donors. Her story was distasteful enough to have credibility.

I hadn't heard from her in a while, so part of me was pleased to see Cass again, yet another part of me was nothing but red flags of concern. I was richer than rich by that point and able to influence elections, but that didn't mean I gave a shit about politics. It was those red flags of concern that made me look around her office with intentionality while we were talking. That's when I saw the picture of Cass, the mayor, and Pat standing with a small group of people. Banners in the background proclaimed, "Narman for Mayor." The Narman election took place eight years ago in 2002! The judge "randomly assigned" me to Pat six years after that in 2008!

Since I hadn't had much to do with Cass during those years, I probably never mentioned Pat to her, and she may not have known to remove their picture from the room before my arrival. Either that or she looked at it so much that she didn't see it anymore and forgot it was there. Be that as it may, I had mentioned Cass to Pat plenty of times, and she never once told me they knew each other. The picture proved they did. It also proved I was in trouble, for in my circles of interaction, there is no such thing as coincidence.

CHAPTER 21

El Perro Loco

Follow but thy star. Thou canst not fail to win the glorious haven
if in glad life your judgement does not falter. Up in the sunlit life,
I lost my way before my years had come to their number.
—Dante Alighieri, from *The Divine Comedy*, "Inferno," Canto XV

I t turns out Pat was not coincidentally assigned to me by the judge. It was all very intentional after all. This is 2016 now, so that was a half dozen years ago when I saw the picture in Cass's office. I have not spoken to either Pat or Cass since then.

I am fifty-eight years old and renting a cabin on an acreage from a woman I've known for decades. It's in the Piney Woods region of North Louisiana. Our only geographic claim to fame is the marker commemorating the ambush on Bonnie and Clyde not far up the road from where I sit this very minute.

I live on the banks of the Cypress Bayou River, which flows south into the Atchafalaya Basin. I have been quite happy here these half dozen years, but something has come up which reminds me of the old days. I have heard mention of Ghibelline. Those memories motivated me to pick up this diary. I'm looking for details about Ghibelline, and I hope I have written something on these pages that will supply those details. I'm also motivated to write and edit. I want to get my story straight. Old habits die hard.

Ariadne is my landlady's name. I could buy everything she owns with the spare change in my bank accounts, but I like our rental arrangement, so I keep it this way. Besides, real estate purchases involve names and legal documentation, but Ariadne prefers her payments in cash without paperwork. Her name means "Most Holy," but everybody calls her "Sunday." She runs a restaurant from her house, literally, and she cooks out of her kitchen. As the crow flies, Sunday's acreage is only about a half-hour drive south of Interstate 20, but as time and people go, it's 1950 and always will be. Some of that is good, and some of it is bad, but either way, this situation suits my daily needs, which is all I ever ask of life these days.

I went into hiding for a lot of reasons, not least among them being that I'm damn tired of humanity. I don't hate people like I once did, but neither do I want to intermingle with a lot of them.

In addition to learning that Cass and Pat know each other, another reason I went into hiding is that we experienced a demoralizing plot against one of the best colleagues in the Club. Uriah was his codename—Uriah the Hittite. If my codename was Mike Stand for my ability to be unnoticed right in front of people like a microphone stand, then his codename was Uriah the Hittite for being honorable in every way. If a guy that good can take a fatal blow to the spine, then the rest of us are in serious trouble. His death proves that if something having influence over you wants to get you, then you're gonna get got. If it can happen to a superstar like Uriah, then a dung beetle like me doesn't stand a chance. An ounce of prevention is worth a pound of cure, so I vaporized into a cash-only rental agreement in rural Louisiana with a woman who doesn't even go by her real name. My days are safe and restful.

I don't want to oversell my seclusion. It's a low-maintenance effort, especially after six years. It's true that I've done some dastardly deeds, but I've not made powerful enemies who are yearning to dig me up. Besides, I'm dangerous in my own weird way, so nobody is going to trifle with me lightly.

I don't want to get in anyone's crossfire, so as long as I stay low and don't interrupt anyone's plans, I should be fine. Nevertheless, trophic cascades in government are never pretty or rational, so some out-of-sight-out-of-mind retreat won't be a bad thing for me, even if it's true that nobody cares about me anymore. The bastards can eat themselves just fine on their own.

People here in the Piney Woods district are friendly and polite but not divulging with newcomers, and we're helpful to travelers but also suspicious of strangers who make conversation by asking questions. Questions from a stranger are equivalent to presumption and trespass, so if you want somewhere to hide, the Piney Woods district is the perfect place—as long as you're a good neighbor. Bad neighbors don't last long. The definition of "good neighbor" is "one who is considerate but otherwise minds his or her own damn business." The meaning of "don't last long" is that nobody sees them anymore. I fit right in here in these parts.

The road that passes Sunday's property is a shortcut road. It has lots of traffic but not many residents, so as such roads tend to go, it's nothing more than an absentminded rush between where people were a little while ago and where they'd rather be right now. A road less traveled is a pleasant, inspirational place, but shortcut roads are the opposite of that, for they are overused into obscurity. As long as I don't delay the flow of traffic, this cutoff road is the perfect place to hide, and it's ironic for a guy nicknamed "Microphone Stand" for my ability to remain unseen in plain sight. Since the concept of a getaway implies actually leaving, hypogeal living here is counterintuitive to anyone's instinct to locate me.

People such as my landlady, Sunday, are what make Louisiana great. When she isn't in the kitchen cooking, she's walking around the house giving directives to her customers. "Lunch is on the stove, so serve yourself. I don't deliver to your house or to your table. I don't take orders or requests. If you have dietary needs, tell your mama and your doctor, but don't tell me. You can eat what I cook, and it's on the stove. Take it or leave it. I don't cook breakfast or supper, so don't come here then. I cook lunch six days a week, but not on Sunday. Sunday is the Lord's day, so don't come here on Sunday. I don't serve breakfast or supper, but I do serve lunch, Monday through Saturday, so you can come here then. It's hot on the stove. Serve yourself."

Sunday's hypercharacterization is a charming loop over and over again for hours on end, and people love every minute of it. Especially me. Her devotion to Christianity borders on superstitious, which adds to her charm. My own Christian faith has been growing lately too, but in a different way. The antonym of "superstitious" would be me. I'm a researcher, empirical and thorough, which means I prefer to investigate outside of my own head, and I don't use my own notions as proof that I'm right.

There's an old joke that Louisiana invented the drive-through restaurant because we're too lazy to get out of our vehicles, but that joke doesn't apply to Sunday's restaurant. Going inside to be with her is half the fun of being a patron. Besides, if you pull up in her driveway and ask her to bring your meal out to your car, you'll probably end up wearing it. So will your car. How Sunday can get away with being so bossy and condescending without driving away her customers, I'll never know. In all my cooking careers, I had only one tiff with a customer, and I never saw him again. I didn't even start it.

"Don't you worry about getting lung cancer?" he asked me. I was standing by my big barbecue grill visiting with some other customers at the time, so his intrusion startled me a little. He must have been a Yankee.

"I don't smoke," I replied.

"Then what do you call all this?" he asked, pointing at the billowing chimney coming out of my barbecue rig. Beyond the abruptness of his tone, I was even more offended by the twinkle in his eyes.

"I call it the oldest cooking technique known to civilized society," I quipped. The look in his eyes may have said "I outsmarted you," but the look in my eyes said "Up yours!" I'd overheard him talking earlier in the event, so I knew he had a fresh case of newdoctoritis from Alabama or Ol' Miss or Texas A&M. I can't tell those places apart, so I'm not sure which he attended. It may even have been Florida State, if you can imagine that. Since I was standing there with a hard-earned PhD of my own from LSU and years of experience using it, I was unimpressed with his credentials. I suspect he thought I was being insubordinate, what with me being just the cook.

I occasionally reflect on my conversation with that young doctor when I watch Sunday interacting with her guests. I surmise that people enjoy her bossiness because they don't have to think when she's around. I've learned that the mark of superior people is the ability to think without losing control of our emotions and the ability to communicate without damaging our relationships, and Sunday has these gifts in abundance. Life is just better when a doyenne like Sunday is near us.

Sunday keeps her ears open while her customers talk to see if there might ever be any mention of me, and she tells me of anything that sounds odd. She calls it "Ear hustle between cellies," whatever that means.

None of Sunday's tableware matches. The only thing that matches is a bunch of strangers sitting at the same table, getting to know each other. The way Sunday prattles at them, they always pull together. People tend to bond when in the presence of a common threat.

Sunday likes to eat and drink, which I enjoy about her company because I like to cook and drink. It's the perfect match. We started out as professional acquaintances in the food service industry—she with her pots and pans, and me with my smoker on wheels. She is many things to me, and I take all of them personally. Sunday is my friend.

When I first rented from Sunday, I paid weekly rent for the cabin, but after a while, we took portions of it out in trade: for every day that I cook supper for her, I don't have to pay rent. It's a simple arrangement. Life with Sunday is like that. It's simple and good.

Part of my rent also includes a lawn-maintenance agreement. Sunday knows I'm a multimillionaire, so she could just let me hire someone else to cut the grass, but she made all the previous tenants cut the grass, and she believes in treating people equally, so she makes me cut the grass. As my friend, she probably has a little fun making me do it. I also think that deep down inside her is the voice of her black-skinned female ancestors who were slaves under the whim of white male plantation owners who probably looked a lot like me. As much as she likes me, she can't—and shouldn't—forget the abuses heaped upon those women. I think their voices push her every bit as much as the voice of Kevin Bruce pushes me.

Soon after I moved here, we were having supper one night—which I cooked, of course—and Sunday was outlining the specific details of my grass-cutting responsibilities. She was explaining the exact point to where I should mow.

"Up to 'bout that crawfish chimney would be enough," she said. Not far from the crawfish chimney were some smallish bushes and baby trees bordering the lawn, so I asked about how to treat them. Amateur dendrologist that I am, I take such things perhaps more seriously than I should.

"Do they bear fruit?" Sunday responded, somewhat sharply.

"I don't see any."

"Then mow them. I curse anything that doesn't bear fruit," she said. Having no children, I took her stance a little personally.

In the middle of a Louisiana summer, Bahia grass grows so quickly you can hear it, so I mow frequently, nearly every day, and always up to the boundary that Sunday established. The profits of my usury have been replaced by the sweat of my brow, and I am as happy as a guilty man can be. I take special care to pause my mower over fruitless bushes and fire ant mounds so I can chop them both to smithereens. My days with the Club were about removing undesirable people, but now I remove fruitless bushes and fire ants. Something in me just needs to make the world a better place by getting rid of the bad stuff.

As crawfish will do, the one Sunday used as a landmark moved its chimney every time we had a heavy rain. Since the new boundary was always to my advantage, I mowed to the revised location and teased Sunday about it.

"A deal's a deal," I playfully insisted. "I'm cutting grass all the way to the crawfish chimney." Sunday has a beautiful laugh. It's honest, and it gives me positive energy.

The crawfish continued to relocate its chimney, and I continued to mow to the new location. Eventually, though, the crawfish moved to my disadvantage, so I ate it.

Sunday established a daily rental rate by dividing my weekly rate by seven. She performed her calculations longhand in my presence, and then she spun the paper around and made me read it. "So as not to confuse you or make you think I'm foolin'," she said. In a world full of multifarious fraud, her simplicity is precious.

"You don't have to let me know every day what you're cookin'," Sunday said, "but tell me ahead of time if you can't cook supper for me so I know when I have to cook for myself. Just give me a list of what you need a day or two early, and I'll have it delivered along with my other supplies."

"Okay, Sunday. It's a deal."

"Nothing too expensive or exotic, though. I know how you get."

"Okay, Sunday."

"You're still in hiding, and I don't want to attract attention."

"Okay, Sunday."

She was really just trying to save a buck, but I had to admit she had good reasoning. Anyone wanting to find me would just have to keep an eye out for shipments of dragon fruit, fiddlehead ferns, or *salsa de chicatanas* ordered by a ramshackle restaurant on the banks of the Cypress Bayou River, and I'd be busted.

Sunday has a wonky-eyed Catahoula leopard cur that follows me around the yard and supervises my work while I mow the grass. His name is Phideaux, but I call him Cyclopes.

"Why do you call him Cyclopes?" Sunday asked me one evening over supper.

"Because he's blind in one eye. By the way, which one is it? I can't always be sure."

"Which one is what?"

"His blind eye."

"The one on the right."

"His right or our right?"

"His right."

"I was thinking it was the other eye."

"No, that's the one he just can't see out of."

Phideaux is a washout from the hog-dog trials just up the road in Winnfield. He's got plenty of heart, but because of his blind eye, he turns away from the hog occasionally, and within hog-dog communities, that's unforgivable. It's a standard born of necessity, for turning away from a Louisiana boar will get a dog killed.

Phideaux also has a torn ACL in his right rear leg, so he often walks on three legs with the injured leg suspended in the air. I speculate his blind eye is congenital, but his torn ligament probably happened on a hog hunt. In addition to calling him "Cyclopes," I sometimes call him "Tripod."

"You call that dog a lot of names," Sunday observed.

Phideaux won me over early in our relationship because soon after I moved to Sunday's cottage, I developed a constant ringing in my ears. Prone to pessimism and self-reproach as I am, I attributed the ringing to damage I had done to my hearing from a life of sinful living, but one day when Phideaux was in the cottage with me and the ringing started, he cocked his head to the side and strolled into the bathroom. I followed him and found him pressing his nose against the back of the toilet. It turned out the float valve needed replacing, and water pressure against the worn diaphragm was making the thing vibrate with a high-pitched song. Phideaux reminded me that sometimes things happen independently of me, and I may be neither the cause nor the audience. Tinnitus is no big deal, but verifying to me that I overestimate my importance and can be a little too hard on myself was priceless.

After I ate the crawfish and had to pick a new landmark to serve as my lawn care boundary, Phideaux looked at me with concern because I mowed to a chimney-free location. He looks like Marty Feldman in *Young Frankenstein* when he tries to think. All he needs is a hump on his back.

One of my favorite pastimes is watching Phideaux chase lizards. They're chameleons, Texas horned, and skinks, mostly. It's fun to watch Phideaux chase them—particularly around Sunday's stacks of smoker wood, because he can dishevel about a rick of oak every time he chases a lizard into the cord. Sunday and I both cook our entrées with real wood whenever it's possible, so she has stacks and stacks of it in storage for her restaurant. In fact, now that I think of it, swapping smoker wood is how we met all those years ago. Gas grills are for sissies.

Phideaux's reptile-chasing habits cost me some security once. He mouthed on a toad and wobbled on semiparalyzed legs for the rest of the day, so I took him to the vet. I've come out of hiding only twice since I've been living here. Taking Phideaux to the doctor was the first time; the second time was to go to the bank to set up an endowment account for no-chance women, but those details will have to wait.

In addition to chasing lizards and mouthing toads, Phideaux loves to scratch his back under the arm of a rocking chair in my cabin. I like it when I'm sitting in the chair, but I always make him quit when the rocking chair is empty, because I heard that rocking an empty chair invites death, bad luck, and evil spirits. Maybe that applies only to people, not dogs; but since the consequence seems so dire, I'm not taking any chances.

I like Phideaux a lot; I just wish he wouldn't lie on the kitchen floor directly behind me while I'm at the counter cooking. I have yet to bust my ass tripping over him, but if I live long enough, it's inevitable.

Phideaux is blue merle and lives with me about half the time. The custody agreement I have with Sunday for Phideaux isn't as precise as the lawn care agreement, so he pretty much is just here when he's here and not here when he's not here. He really is lovely, particularly when he strikes one of his wise, noble poses. I tried for the longest time when I first moved here to take his picture when he does that, but I've since given up. The little freak will hold the most photographic position imaginable right up until I aim my cell phone at him, and then he curls around and licks his balls.

Blind eye or not, Phideaux keeps those two beautiful baby-blue peepers aimed straight at me the whole time I'm around him. I've heard it said that the glass eyes of a Catahoula leopard cur will make you examine your very soul, and if my experience with Phideaux means anything, then the saying is true. Maybe that's why he deserves so much ink here in my diary. It also shows how small my life has become. I'm happy this way, and I want to write about it.

Having lost Pat as my counsellor, I lean on Phideaux for companionship and therapy. I lean on Sunday too, I guess. She has been instrumental in my redemption. They both have. They have softened my heart substantially over these past half dozen years.

Tranquility notwithstanding, once in a while something happens that is neither inconsequential nor common nor fair. It lands squarely upon us, and we feel that it's important enough to get involved and take action, even if it's uncomfortable or violent. Sometimes God wants us strong, silent types to stop being quiet and humble and open a can of whoop-ass on the bad guys of the world.

My turning point into action and redemption was a drug called Ghibelline. I always thought it was a mockable label, sounding like a swamp-culture recipe that mixed poke sallet, Hoover hogs, and sunchokes.

In the cool of the evenings, Sunday and I eat outside. The cabin I rent from her has a screened porch on the back, so even in the rain we can sit there. The more she drinks, the more she talks, and during some of our conversations, she mentioned Ghibelline. Every time she did, it rang a deep, distant gong in the back of my brain. I remember these moments well.

Sunday and Phideaux are the perfect cohorts. If you're going underground and could use a little redemptive therapy, spending the day with Phideaux and the evening with Sunday is exactly the thing to do. All good things come to an end.

CHAPTER 22

House of Him that Hath His Shoe Loosed

There is a place low down, not known to sight but only sound. It has a hollow
channel, and through a devious course its wandering waters creep.
—Dante Alighieri, from *The Divine Comedy*, "Inferno," canto X

S unday certainly isn't the first person who mentioned Ghibelline
to me, but she is the one who gave it to me in context—a
human context. Actually, I first heard of Ghibelline through
my involvement with the Club and with Cass being on the city
council. The mention back then was of third-party references in a
scientific context, so it lacked a vulnerable framework. I was busy
with my own salient plans in those days and not inclined to butt heads
with things that didn't involve me, so I didn't pay much attention to
the Ghibelline conversations—not back then.

Sunday talks a lot about her family—deaths mostly. She is as
old as the hills, so talking about a lot of dead people shouldn't be
unusual, but the thing that caught my attention was the ages of the
people who died. They were young—nearly all infants or children.
Dozens of them.

Sunday said the doctors gave young mothers a drug to calm
their nerves after each child was born, and the drug seemed to work,
because women relaxed when they took it. She said it was popular
throughout the whole community because people started taking it

like crazy, prescription or not. Mothers took it, fathers took it, teenage boys took it, and grandparents and aunts and uncles took it. Everyone passed it around as if it were candy. As she talked, I remembered what Obra taught me about noticing what isn't there and what doesn't happen. It inspired me to think about Ghibelline and remember the early conversations I had disregarded.

Something about this topic wasn't passing the stink test. For starters, why were supplies of Ghibelline in these communities so abundant? People here couldn't get so much as an aspirin for free, yet providers turned a blind eye to Ghibelline abuses and prescribed it by the bucketful.

I had come to know these people and their families. In addition to what Sunday said, their appearance was part of what tipped me off that something was wrong. They were placid but not peaceful, as if there was an angry person inside of a calm body. One evening at supper, Sunday said the drug's name to me. "Jibling," she called it. Her mispronunciation is what caused me to not associate her conversations with my early knowledge of Ghibelline. Finally I connected the dots.

"I've heard that before," I told her. "Or something like that."

"Back when you were out?"

"Yeah. It was a funny name like that one, but that's not the one. Not exactly, anyway. I'll have to think about it when I'm sober. Remind me."

"Okay," Sunday said, and she then continued with her story. "I told my daughter that name sounds like chicken innards. 'Jibling.' Don't that sound stupid? My daughter said it sounds like a game for kids. I never took Jibling myself. Don't know why. Just never did. Never got around to it, I guess."

And just like that, these thoughts joined in my mind: the poke sallet and Hoover hogs and sunchokes in my memory, the chicken innards in Sunday's imagination, and the game for children in her daughter's thoughts. They all merged, casually at first—a sashay, an allemande, a gavotte. But then, suddenly, there it all was, crystal clear. Kevin Bruce was screaming inside my rye-addled brain. "Wake up! Pay attention!" It was just as Pat said all those years ago—late processing.

Ghibelline was being used for genocide. My imagination was in full roil, but not in the usual drifty way. Memories and logic and scientific information were coming together in my head.

The scientific process behind Ghibelline's influence is that Mother Nature created a polypeptide hormone called oxytocin. Its nickname is the parenting hormone—PH for short. By whatever name, PH is the thing that makes an otherwise sane person go crazy with desire to have a child, and then be so full of love and devotion for the baby that they go batshit ebullient to serve and protect it.

Without PH, the human race would end. That hormone is the very thing Ghibelline is designed to dissolve. Without PH, we would not desire to have children, or to tend to their needs if we managed to have them by accident. We would not get out of bed to tend a sickly baby, and we would not keep our children safe until they were old enough to do it for themselves. Selectively administered, Ghibelline could thin the population one neighborhood at a time. Governments around the world would be lining up secretly to buy it for use against international enemies—and their own groups of unwanted citizens.

I hated the concept of genocide. True, I had killed so many people while I was working for the Club that I couldn't remember them all, but they were all people who, by their own individual behaviors and sustained choices, proved themselves to be deleterious to others. I did not ever kill a group without first knowing who was in it or how they had behaved prior to that.

When I first learned of Ghibelline from the Club, the drug was in the advanced stages of refinement. Considering that our central purpose was to remove undesirables in undetectable ways, a drug like Ghibelline could be valuable to us; however, its researchers had to find an antidote just in case the thing got out of hand. After all, the plan was to thin the population selectively, not exterminate it, and the people who intended to implement Ghibelline wanted to keep the thing under control. They had enough sense to know that Pandora's box isn't a carton of seasoning you can sprinkle to your exact taste and then quit; it's a balls-to-the-wall hullabaloo of uncontrollable excess followed by chaos and apocalypse.

Arcane research was fine-tuning Ghibelline so it could be totally effective on some groups of people but inconsequential to the rest. Ghibelline began as pure science without so much as a touch of immorality, right up until the point when project managers started deciding who should get struck by lightning and who should remain unscathed.

CHAPTER 23

Fire Followers Flowers

If thou learn of this and keep from tears, then thou art right cruel.
If thou for this weep not, at what then art thou wont to weep?
—**Dante Alighieri**, from ***The Divine Comedy***, **"Inferno," canto XXXIII**

Ghibelline was originally designed to diminish postpartum depression in women, but it revealed a ghastly side effect. Beta tests showed that Ghibelline kept women calm all right, but it did it to an extreme—so much so that it eliminated their protective mothering instinct altogether!

Ghibelline doesn't make mothers harm their children outright; it just makes them not care one way or another. The child mortality rate among beta test women who took Ghibelline was astronomical, so it warranted further study. That study turned villainous.

Ghibelline wasn't designed for infanticide; it just happened that way. Making caregivers disregard their children was unexpected. Even the drug's makers were surprised.

Early references for Ghibelline codenamed it "the dinosaur drug." As code names go, this was a good one; not only did it hide the real identity of the thing it labeled, but it also distracted potential investigators off the trail, because the word "dinosaur" implies something so ancient that it is now immaterial and irrelevant.

The code name "dinosaur drug" is actually a metaphor based on one of the theories of dinosaur extinction. That particular theory conjectures dinosaurs became extinct not because of something that killed living dinosaurs but because something happened to prevent new generations of dinosaurs. Eventually all the living dinosaurs died, and since there were no young dinosaurs to replace them, the entire species became extinct.

Theoretically, if somebody wanted to exterminate dinosaurs but for whatever reason couldn't just outright kill them, this would be the perfect plan. The same goes for eradicating subgroups of people—ergo, "the dinosaur drug."

My greatest motivation against Ghibelline is knowing that however messed up humanity may be, we begin anew with fresh hope and a clean start every time a baby is born. This is pure logic to me. I have no gushing hormones, and I don't need a hug. I'm dwelling on these paragraphs to be clear that I am not a crusader. I never was and never will be. As any combat veteran will tell you, the farther out front you get, the more you're vulnerable to friendly fire, and I had been out front for much of my life.

Yet with all that having been said, here I am, attempting to protect snot-nosed kids from being neglected by their drug-induced, pococurante parents. Amazing!

The thing is designed to kill kids, I thought to myself. I may have even murmured the words out loud. I'm not sure, but Phideaux cocked his head just then. Maybe he felt me processing a powerful thought.

You'd think my realization about Ghibelline would deserve an exclamation point, but I decided not to use one as I wrote those words because the thought didn't make any more noise in my mind than the smooth sounds of a cardboard puzzle piece clicking gently into place to form a picture. I can feel Kevin Bruce at work in my brain.

I had my moment of epiphany less than a week ago. I dwelt upon it as Sunday left me after our meal that evening to walk up the path to her house.

Self-appointed tutelary that I am, it's a nightly ritual for me to watch Sunday leave each evening after we have supper. After she goes into her house, I sit and drink alone with Phideaux for the hour or so that her end-of-day hygiene process requires. First I watch her flashlight bob and weave up the path and I listen for the back door of her house to open and close, and then I watch for the lights in her house to come on and go off, in leapfrog sets of two, as she passes through the hallways and rooms, ending in her bedroom. Her nightly departure inspires my guardian sensibilities, so I pay attention not only to be sure she is safe but also because I enjoy overwatching her. I know how much time she needs to take her to take her pills, feed the bird in the kitchen, use the bathroom, read her Bible verses in bed, pray, and then turn out the last lamp. Being her security guard isn't part of our rental arrangement. I do it instinctively.

Sunday and I have a routine of finishing supper each night with a glass of rye whiskey, so we each have a little buzz when she leaves. I enjoy that time of day very much and look forward to it. It is my quiet time, come rain or come shine. The night when I had my serendipitous epiphany about Ghibelline was no different. A few days later, as we were sipping our rye, I asked her a question.

"Miss Ariadne, I'm curious about something." It was rare for me to use her real name.

"Go on, child," Sunday said. She didn't usually speak to me so nurturingly, but she could feel the stock brewing in my spirit.

"Why are there so few men around here?" I asked.

"They're off chasing their easy star," she said. "We all want to be great. A star athlete or a star musician or a movie star—or any other kind of star, I guess, as long as we get rich and famous." She chuckled a little. "We all try to grab an easy star at some point—some people more than others. Mostly, we grab for it when we're young. Most folks are willing to work for their goals a little after we grow up, but some people never get over that immature yearning for an easy star. They figure they deserve it, and if it's not here, then it must be somewhere else, so they set off looking for it. They just can't quit wandering, no matter what happens to them or the people who need them.

"I ain't judging though," Sunday said to me with a quick turn of her face toward mine. I felt she was aiming those dark eyes of hers at me for emphasis, so I paid close attention. "It sounds like I'm judging, but all I'm doin' is answerin' your question, plain and simple, and

I don't mean no more than that. I done some things ma'self that I ain't proud of, and I earned me a name that ain't exactly welcome in all parts. What I'm sayin' is wantin' an easy star is a sickness that drives some people. A lot of men from here seem to have it—more than most other places." Sunday paused and reflected for a moment. "My man included. It's like they just don't think of anything but that star—the easy star."

She called her man "Ugolino" by the way. It was a rare piece of sarcasm from Sunday. She usually spoke in much more concrete terms. I'm sure he deserved her insolence. She said that if it were up to him, her children would have starved to death. I don't know the whereabouts of Sunday's husband. For all I know, the Club deeded him. Judging by his legacy, it's a rational probability.

"Did Ugolino ever take Ghibelline?" I asked, perhaps a little suddenly.

"Yes," she said. "By the handful. He got it from my oldest daughter when she had her first baby, the one that died. Why do you ask?"

Sunday may not have known what caused adults to wander off chasing easy stars or parents to not care about their children, but I knew. It wasn't genetic, and it wasn't a character flaw; it was a pharmaceutical, and it had a name—Ghibelline!

Ghibelline takes years to work, and even then, it's indirect. It's the perfect murder weapon because Joe and Sally Blow sitting in a jury box can't discern something that abstract or overreaching. Most folks need a nice, tidy package of information, and if not for my training all those years ago with Obra, I would probably still be in that mindset.

I know it sounds hokey, but on that one particular night when Sunday told me about the easy star, I had a weird dream. Even weirder than the dream itself is the fact that I remember it so clearly—I was in charge of a sinking ship.

The ship was small, with only a few dozen passengers onboard. It was so small that there was only one lifeboat, which could carry exactly ten people. My precise knowledge of that number is important, because my job was to decide who lived and who drowned.

All the passengers stood before me, pleading their cases. For the second time in my life, I understood God—at least a little better—because I didn't pick the most righteous or the most reverent or the sweetest or the kindest or the most innocent. I didn't even pick the ones who were the best apple polishers, obsequiously propitiating me. What I picked were the ones who seemed the most likely to survive the experiences of hardship that lay ahead. Wouldn't anything else have been futile? Wouldn't I have been a fool to fill a lifeboat with people who couldn't take it to shore or wouldn't regenerate life once they got there?

That was the second time I understood God a little better. The first time was only a few years earlier, and the insight was equally powerful. It happened while I was tutoring some of Sunday's friends and family on the screened porch of my cottage, and one of the very brightest among them accused me of being unfair.

My instruction to the group was informal and very certainly for free. It started out with a conversation but eventually evolved into a sort of impromptu one-room-schoolhouse situation for the neighborhood. Their ages spanned decades, all the way from children to octogenarians. I enjoyed it. We did that for probably less than a year, then it evaporated.

The student who felt unfairly put upon was perhaps my favorite. She had seen me giving answers to the others, and she wanted to know why I was making her labor for her solutions. She wanted the same courtesy of ease I had given to the others. That's when it hit me, my first little clarity about God, for I realized her observation was valid, but it was backward. It was to her I gave my best services, not the others.

To the students who wouldn't benefit from my instruction I gave quick fixes, knowing they would be done with the occasion and move along forgetfully regardless of whatever I did. But to the students who were capable of erudition, I found myself requiring an arduous journey of discovery and learning. I knew they would benefit from the process as much as from the result. They would profit from the experience, and my instructional efforts would not be wasted on them. A huge part of me stopped resenting God when I had that first moment of epiphany, because I realized I had been chosen for a journey of learning. Another part of me stopped resenting God with this second epiphany in my dream because I realized God is about the future, not the past.

On the deck of that sinking ship in my dream, people stood before me in a mare's nest of clamor, protesting as a group but pleading as individuals. They all talked at once, yet I could hear them singularly, and very clearly. That part was odd, for among all that din, I could perceive each of their separate voices.

They didn't attack me or use force of any kind to try to get into the lifeboat. All they did was talk. It was as if I was untouchable and unquestionable, and the only way they could make it into that lifeboat was to have me put them there. I don't know why I felt omnipotent and immune, but I did, and I don't know why my permission to get on that lifeboat was ineluctable, but it was.

Their reasons were compelling, but the people were simpleminded, for I was studying them for useful future attributes, not for their arguments. I watched their behaviors waaaaaay more than I listened to their admonitions.

I felt the ship drop lower into the water, and I knew our time was short. I saw the jetsam fling and the flotsam rise. I looked for courageous eyes and strong arms, and for nubile, lusty women who would fly into those strong arms, eager to breed new generations. I watched for clear minds and robust spirits. I looked for variety as much as I could—of race and ethnicity and age and inclination and ideology—because I didn't want one weakness to kill them all.

Everything I looked for was about the future, not the past. I keenly felt the burden of my decisions, yet I did not waffle in my thinking. It was quite a dream.

I don't remember whom I picked to get into that lifeboat, but I do remember two clear impressions at the end. Those two things are extremely clear in my mind, as if they were happening right now, this very minute, in front of my eyes.

The first thing I remember is that the lifeboat departed without me, and that by not getting on it, I had sealed my own death. *Bacio della morte.* I remember watching the lifeboat push off from the ship and hearing the tholes of the oars strain in their holes on the gunwale to row away from the rest of us. The sound was a heavy, lumbering creak.

The second very clear thing I remember is that the lifeboat had two empty seats. My judgment about the passengers was pluperfect, and I felt no compulsion to fill the boat to capacity. Adding two more people would have weakened the cooperation and effectiveness of the eight members already on board.

Maybe the dream was just from the rye I drank, or maybe it was a genuine moment of epiphany sent from God and Kevin Bruce. I don't know, but still, I can't forget it. Even if it was just a rye-soaked experience, it was still insightful.

When Sunday arrived the next evening for supper, I asked more questions about Ghibelline. It was a conversation leading to my ultimate redemption. I told Sunday it was important for me to get that information from her daughters and their friends.

"Let's bring them all together," she said. "We'll do it Saturday night, right here. The next day is Easter, so all the women will be here together, and I'll check with the ones from out of town just to be sure they'll come. We can sit around to talk; that way you can get your facts." Even as she said the words, I saw myself in my dream sending that lifeboat away without getting into one of its two empty seats.

CHAPTER 24

Achan the Opportunist

A remembrance to him comes—how foolish Achan purloined the spoil and incurred Joshua's wrath. Keeping this in mind, forward he goes, unarmed but with a better knowledge of himself and his friends.
—Dante Alighieri, from *The Divine Comedy*, "Inferno," canto XX

"Man's been comin' around lately!" Sunday barked at me this morning, out of the blue. Today is Saturday. Yesterday was Good Friday. Tomorrow is Easter. Tonight is our supper with the women in Sunday's circle.

I can always tell when a topic has been weighing heavily on Sunday's mind because she'll hit me with it all at once. She's like that. I've observed that when something concerns her, she lets it well up inside until she can't contain it anymore, and then it shoots out of her mouth with a punch. That's her telltale giveaway.

"Okay" is all I said. I could tell in her eyes she knew this news hit me hard. My giveaway is to minimize my reaction when I hear things that are important.

I guess I always knew this day would come. I've been especially aware of it lately because Sunday's invitation to supper was to discuss Ghibelline. News like that travels. The guy Sunday told me about is most likely here because of those conversations. One of two things will happen: he'll want to quiet the chatter or he'll want a piece of the action. Either way, he's dangerous, because nothing about Ghibelline invites betterment. Apparently today is the day I knew would come.

"Did he ask questions?" I asked Sunday when she told me about the guy. Her eyes visibly calmed a little when I said that to her. I think she was comforted because I spoke words. When I'm upset, I don't talk.

"Not with his mouth," she answered. That was the worst information she could give me, because it meant this guy was a pro. "His eyes did the talkin'," she added. My torso tightened, probably visibly. I didn't have much to say for the rest of the afternoon. I prefer to do manual labor when I'm in that kind of mood. Busy hands comfort me.

Sure enough, an uninvited guy sauntered into the backyard a few hours later and started talking. I was splitting red oak firewood. Phideaux watched me work. I didn't notice the guy at first, but the dog did. He perked, so I followed his gaze.

"Can I help you?" I asked the guy.

"How you doin'?" was his reply.

I hate when people do that—answer a question with a question. It either means they're so stupid that they can't process what another person says or they're planning to handle the situation so thoroughly that they disregard the inquiry. I don't like either option.

"What can I do for you?" I asked as a follow-up.

"You doin' all right?"

There it was again! This was clearly the guy Sunday told me about. I studied his eyes. They weren't stupid, which meant his brain could handle what his ears delivered. Option two must be the one that fit him. Following my either-or reasoning about questions and answers, this meant he was intending to control our conversation. *No worries—he might work in door-to-door sales, and this could be his overrehearsed opening sequence. Either that or he has to die. This conversation can go one way or the other. Better for him if he works in sales. I haven't killed anyone in quite a long while, and I'm jonesin' for a homicide.*

"The restaurant is up front," I said to the guy. "That's where they conduct business, so whatever you're selling, that's the place to do it." I turned my back on him and started splitting red oak with the axe again. A real pro would have noticed I kept my eyes on the dog.

Phideaux stood to all fours and focused behind me, so I spun roundhouse style and connected the axe into the guy's torso as he came up to attack me from the rear. The look of amazement on his face almost matched the shock I saw in Riner Salse's eyes years ago when I shoved him back through the door at Wolf's.

For an assassin, this guy didn't command much agility. He pretty much just stopped in his tracks and stood there when he saw me spin around. I speculate he was trying to think of something to say. Not all situations can be handled with words.

I'm out of practice, and I used way too much force on the axe, so it stuck in the guy's ribs up to the wooden handle. I had to hick him off of it before I could use it to split his face and neck with several more follow-up whacks. The sound of the axe on his skull was similar to the noise of splitting of red oak firewood, so I doubt anyone in the house up front even noticed the difference.

It's a bad idea to attack someone who has a dog and an axe. Turns out this guy wasn't much of a pro after all, for a more skillful assassin would have known to wait for a better opportunity. He must have been on his second murder.

I pulled his wallet out of his pants and looked at his ID. His name was Achan. I wrapped his body in garbage bags and old rugs, and then I wrestled him into the trunk of my car and continued to split red oak firewood for Sunday, all the while wondering what Kevin Bruce was thinking about this situation. Was he pleased that I had returned to my former glory, or was he upset that I fell off the murder-abstinence wagon? Phideaux curled into a ball and went back to sleep. He's getting old and starting to show his age.

CHAPTER 25

The Last Supper

But night now ascends, and it is time for parting …
All has been seen. Now my powers can rest from this high fantasy.
**—Dante Alighieri, from *The Divine Comedy*, "Inferno,"
canto XXXIV, and "Paradiso," canto XXXIII**

At the start of this diary, I was searching for a purpose, so I punched a total stranger in the throat to defend a woman I didn't know. Could that really have been a decade ago?

I now know clearly about Ghibelline. It gives me aim. I am not confused any longer. I know what I must do.

I don't have a lot of respect for humanity, yet here I am, willing to sacrifice myself for parents and their families. I don't even know the people I'm saving, but I do know I have to save them from this horrible drug, just as I knew I had to defend that waitress in a parking lot. What else am I to do—turn my back on an evil thing when I alone am best qualified to put a stop to it?

I've enjoyed reading my diary these past few days. It would make a great novel if only I had some skills as a storyteller. I tried writing a book once, but the only thing I ended up with was the most thoroughly edited first page in all literary history. After a couple of years and no second page, I gave up. Between my laziness and Kevin Bruce's glacial deliveries of inspiration, it would have taken us decades to write a novel.

Great writing has to be germane to art and life somehow, but I am still too much of a loner to deserve that vision. Nobody who sees the strife and heartache of other people as being unrelatable can ever achieve greatness. Great art always has to communicate a problem that afflicts all people—past, present, and future. Everything else is fugazi, no matter how much it pays. Mountebanks may achieve a position of comfort and advantage, but so does a full-bellied lounge of lizards sunning on a summit rock. Through strife and earned victory, human life actualizes its greatest meaning, but the culmination of that meaning into a work of art requires fellowship, and I have none.

I am through with my diary now, bringing it to a close. No one will ever read it, but then, that was never the point. I have intentionally pretended to be writing to an audience because the process was more therapeutic for me that way. When I write only to myself, I end up with a kind of lazy shorthand, creating tautologies and pleonasms mostly. Still, in the back of my mind I harbor a lingering stargaze that somehow my diary may turn into something good for other people—that someone will read it and find my experience to be helpful.

Even without renown, I take comfort knowing that, here and there, God smiled upon Kevin Bruce and me. We gratefully and gladly leave it at that, not because of humility, but because of common sense. We have seen too much to be fooled. *Deus gignit artifex; Diaboli creat fama.*

It is late Saturday night as I sit here in the screened porch on the back of my cabin, sipping rye whiskey with Phideaux. The women have left, and I am at my old writing desk, spotlighted in the darkness by my little green banker's lamp. Except for Phideaux, I am alone, enjoying my dulcet mood. The piney woods of North Louisiana smell wonderful at this time of night. I am feeling gruntled, which is rare.

The hour is so late on Saturday night that it may now be early Sunday morning. Time travels in loops back upon itself to be so late that we can be early once again. Life regenerates and goes on that way.

If this is Sunday, then it is Easter Sunday. The women departed hours ago. The sound of women's laughter has always uplifted me, and they had plenty of it. Judging by the feral quality of their singing while they walked out the door and up the path, they were happy. They will drive to church together at sunrise, new hats and all.

Loner that I am, I have always been attracted to life's bycatch moments. Because of that, I will remember these women leaving the party far more mightily than I will remember anything they actually did while at the party.

The women drank quite a lot this evening. They were celebrating because I put my entire wealth into a donor-advised trust account supporting Sunday's church. Earlier in my life, I witnessed the ill effects of windfall money on people who aren't experienced enough to manage the abundance of abrupt wealth, so I set this money into an endowment and designated the withdrawals as interest-only sources of revenue over time. The principal is enormous, so the interest income is going to last for a long, long while to help women in Sunday's community who never had a chance.

The more the women drank at my house to celebrate, the more they talked about sex. It was hilarious! I gormandized them, and they courted me flirtingly as payment.

"You a good cook, Dr. Anthony," one of the women said to me. She was large and happy, with a gift of comedic leadership. The others always agreed with what she said.

Sunday introduced me by my title and last name, and these women have used it throughout our time together. Something about the way they said it was cozy. Considering the respect I have for each of these women, it seems suitable to have them call me by my title and last name.

"Come hungry, eat plenty, and wear comfortable clothes because you're going to fling a little," I said in response to their compliments. "And I'm not just talking about my cooking," I added with a wink.

"*Ooh!* Now there's a man who knows women." They all laughed.

"Dr. Anthony, what was your first experience—you know, with a girl?" the big woman asked me. An immediate hush overfell the room in anticipation of my answer.

"I found some pictures under a shed beside some railroad tracks," I answered. They all laughed again.

"That ain't what I'm talkin' about. Pictures don't count. I mean with a live person."

"The pictures were better," I said. The women howled. They had no idea I was telling the truth.

There they all were, those wonderful women in my cabin—my home. The sourpuss and the schemer, the daredevil and the dreamer. All of one quintessence and accord.

Sunday and the women were wonderful tonight. They were just what I needed, and as I sit here alone on my screened porch reading my diary and petting Phideaux's ears, I smile at the memory of them. As Seder meals go, we had a good one, irreverent though it might have been.

Even though these women have only recently left, I miss them terribly. Lord, how I wish I could look in the rearview mirror of my life every day and see them there behind me. Oh how that would bolster me, here in my Gethsemane on the banks of the Cypress Bayou.

My last supper with Sunday and the women was a success. In addition to achieving my fact-finding goals about Ghibelline, the gathering was a delight. A dozen women attended. I ate crawfish until my tail-squeezing thumb got so sore I had to quit.

As I sit here on my porch, I listen to the tutti polyphonic music of the dark-hours bayou. If ever there was a stage for a world-class librettist, nighttime in the backwater is it. This is Mother Nature's Tresillo Habanera with a backbeat of Afro-Cuban clave. It's beautiful. I sit sideways to my desk with one arm stretched across the top of its rounded front edge. I absentmindedly play with a pen in my hand and occasionally turn on my creaky wooden chair to lean over the diary and write these last few ontological words.

I watch the screens on my little porch breathe in and out as a million hungry insects push against them, trying to get through to eat me. I am brazenfaced, impertinently cocooned within the safety of my porch. My every exhalation makes a taunting, vaporish, warm-blooded image that wafts incautiously out into the black-night air. This is no small risk I am taking, for even though they are tiny, these creatures are dangerous. Many more people die from viruses than from bears. If you want to die mysteriously, just go out on a bayou for a stroll at night and have yourself a casual look around. Soon you'll get your wish. Trust me, for I know these things.

My old wooden swivel chair creaks under my weight, punctuating the deep-throated croaking of bullfrogs nearby, egging them on. Clinking ice in my sweaty highball glass inspires nighttime peepers to chirp. I am their drunken conductor, and they my talented musicians.

In but a few weeks, or maybe even days, this porch will be a *schvitz*, too damn hot for people even in the middle of the night like this. Late-spring humidity in Louisiana is like termination dust in Alaska. Everything stops. But now, Easter Sunday weekend, summer heat has yet to drive us back inside to our mechanically conditioned air.

I normally have more sense than to sit in bug-infested, witchy North Louisiana air so thick with pine pollen that it looks like a foggy mist, but I've probably not many nights remaining to live, so I tarry here, pridefully and imprudently. I've not long to worry about health or any of that sort of thing, so here and now, I choose to filibuster against life's mundane maladies and the commonsense behaviors designed to prevent them.

Here I take my stand. Here, at this time and in this place, I raise my own Ebenezer. My own stone of help. My own monument for future generations, brought about by divine intervention.

I'm honored to have received my burning-bush message, but I also know that being recognized by God comes with a price—and rightfully so. The higher the calling, the greater the cost. History is replete with examples. Soon that list will include me, unspoken though my membership may be.

My duties are clear. I embark tomorrow, Easter Sunday, beginning my quest to find and kill the creators and distributors of Ghibelline. *Vexilla Regis prodeunt inferni*, with Achan's body in my trunk. I need to deliver him to the people who sent him. I need to flush them out and cause them to reveal themselves with knee-jerk reactions when they panic at the sight of his axe-hacked face.

I promise to come back and write about my exploits if I survive, so if there are no further entries in this diary, that means I'm dead. If I survive, I will return to write, for I will need to continue the logline of meaning this diary has given me. If there is no additional writing after this, then I have been killed. *Ars moriendi. Mort de rire.*

If I die, rest assured I died as a hero. Not all heroes get public medals, but I believe God sees quiet acts of heroism with extra clarity. That's a pretty good audience. *Sic incipit vita nova.*

Epilogue

Beatrice Portinari looks up from reading the diary. She thinks this guy is either brilliant or crazy. She's not sure which, but she decides to invest a little more time to find out. She enjoys his playfully sarcastic overcharacterizations, so she reads on, but she then stops reading and flips the old diary closed with a jerk of her forearms to examine the cover. She keeps one of her thumbs between the pages to hold her place. This is a large diary—large enough that she holds it in both hands at once.

Beatrice is in New Orleans at a used bookstore on Decatur Street. This is Thursday evening. Tomorrow is Good Friday, and she has come into the city to deliver her two children to her ex-husband for their annual Easter visit.

She likes the diary and looks for a price but doesn't see one. She wonders how much the bookstore is going to charge and whether she should bother to ask. She again opens the diary and continues reading.

She stands as she reads, leaning her shoulder against a towering bookcase, her face bowed into the pages of the diary. She occasionally shifts her weight from one foot to the other, slipping off her low-heeled shoes, one at a time, to absentmindedly rub her toes against the backs of her ankles.

She selected the old diary from a shelf at random because she likes the way it looks. It has the kind of nobility that comes with having stood the test of time.

Beatrice Portinari has no idea how this diary is about to change her life.